"We have to get out of the building."

Jocelyn took out her cell from her cargo pants and whistled low for Maverick to follow her out. The K-9 growled low to argue, but he'd obey. He always obeyed when it counted. Someone had planted a device in the police station. She needed full response.

"What?" Baker asked. "I can't just leave, Carville. In case you weren't aware, I'm the only officer on shift today."

They didn't have time for bickering. She latched on to his uniform collar and rushed to the front of the station with Baker in tow. "We have to go!"

Fire and sharp debris exploded across her back.

Jocelyn slammed into the nearest wall.

The world went dark.

K-9 DETECTION

———

NICHOLE SEVERN

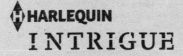

HARLEQUIN
INTRIGUE

For you.

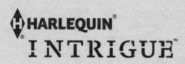

HARLEQUIN®
INTRIGUE™

Recycling programs
for this product may
not exist in your area.

ISBN-13: 978-1-335-59146-3

K-9 Detection

Harlequin Enterprises ULC
22 Adelaide St. West, 41st Floor
Toronto, Ontario M5H 4E3, Canada
www.Harlequin.com

Printed in U.S.A.

Nichole Severn writes explosive romantic suspense with strong heroines, heroes who dare challenge them and a hell of a lot of guns. She resides with her very supportive and patient husband, as well as her demon spawn, in Utah. When she's not writing, she's constantly injuring herself running, rock climbing, practicing yoga and snowboarding. She loves hearing from readers through her website, www.nicholesevern.com, and on Facebook at nicholesevern.

Books by Nichole Severn

Harlequin Intrigue

New Mexico Guard Dogs

K-9 Security
K-9 Detection

Defenders of Battle Mountain

Grave Danger
Dead Giveaway
Dead on Arrival
Presumed Dead
Over Her Dead Body
Dead Again

A Marshal Law Novel

The Fugitive
The Witness
The Prosecutor
The Suspect

Visit the Author Profile page at Harlequin.com.

CAST OF CHARACTERS

Jocelyn Carville—Socorro logistics coordinator Jocelyn Carville has reason to believe a device planted by the vicious *Sangre por Sangre* cartel was meant to destroy evidence in a murder investigation—but convincing the grumpy chief of police becomes a mission in and of itself.

Baker Halsey—Chief of police Baker Halsey doesn't trust private military contractors. But as the investigation comes to a standstill, he'll have to turn to the enthusiastic operative intent on tearing down his guard...before the syndicate strikes again.

Socorro Security—The Pentagon's war on drugs has pulled the private military contractors of Socorro Security into the fray to dismantle the *Sangre por Sangre* cartel...forcing its operatives to risk their lives and their hearts in the process.

Marc De Leon—Suspected of hiring someone from within the cartel to plant the bomb that destroyed the police station, Marc is the only one who can give up *Sangre por Sangre*'s motives...if Jocelyn and Baker can find him.

Driscol Jones—Socorro's combat controller is all too familiar with explosive ordinance in the field, but as the cartel turns its sights on his team, Driscol finds himself back in the middle of a war zone.

Chapter One

She was making the world a better place one cookie at a time.

And there was nothing that said *I'm sorry that your deputy ended up being a traitorous bastard working for the cartel* than her cranberry-lemon cookies.

Jocelyn Carville parked her SUV outside of Alpine Valley's police station. If you could even call it that. In truth, it was nothing more than two double-wide trailers shoved together to look like one long building. The defining boundary between the two sections cut right down the middle with a set of stairs on each side. One half for the courts, and the other for Alpine Valley's finest.

A low groan registered from the back seat, and she glanced at her German shepherd, Maverick, in the rearview mirror. "Don't give me that pitiful look. I saw you steal four cookies off the counter before I wrapped them. You're not getting any more."

Collecting the plate of perfectly wrapped sweets, Jocelyn shouldered out of the vehicle. Maverick pawed at the side door. Anywhere these cookies went, he was sure to follow. Though sometimes she could convince him they were actually friends. He was prickly at best and standoffish at worst. Good thing she knew how to handle both. His nails ticked at the pavement as he jumped free of the SUV.

"Jocelyn Carville." The low register in that voice added an extra twist in her stomach. Chief of Police Baker Halsey had come out of nowhere. Speaking of *prickly*. The man pulled his keys from his uniform slacks, hugging the material tight to his thigh. And what a thigh it was. Never mind the rest of him with his dark hair, deep brown eyes or the slight dent at the bridge of his nose telling her he'd broken it in the past. Nope. She'd take just his thigh if he were offering. "Here I was thinking my day had started off pretty good. What's Socorro want this time?"

A tendril of resentment wormed through her, but she shut it down fast. There wasn't any room to let feelings like that through. Jocelyn readjusted her hold on the plastic-wrapped plate, keeping her head high. "I'm here for you."

Maverick pressed one side of his head against her calf and took a seat. His heat added to the sweat already breaking out beneath her bra. She was former military. It was her job to call on resources to aid in whatever situation had broken out and stay calm while doing it. To look at pain and suffering logically and offer the most beneficial solution possible. She was a damn good logistics coordinator. Most recently in the Pentagon's war on the Sangre por Sangre cartel. Delivering cookies shouldn't spike her adrenaline like this.

Baker pulled up short of the ancient wood stairs leading up to the front door of the station's trailer. "For *me*?"

"I brought you some cookies." Offering him the plate, she pasted on a smile—practically mastered over the years. Just like her cookies. "They're cranberry-lemon with a hint of drizzle. I remember you liked my lemon bread at the town Christmas bake sale last year. I thought you might like these, too."

"Cookies." He stared down at the plate. One second. Two. Her arms could only take the weight for so long. Lucky for her, she didn't have to wait more than a minute. Because the chief walked right up those stairs without another word.

Maybe *prickly* wasn't the right word. A couple more descriptors came to mind, but her mama would wash her mouth out with soap if she ever heard Jocelyn say them out loud. Well, if her mama made an effort to talk to her at all.

She didn't bother calling Maverick as she hiked up the three rickety steps to the station's glass door and ripped it open. Her K-9 partner was always in hot pursuit of any chance of cookies.

This place looked the same as always. Faux wood paneling on the walls, an entire bank of filing cabinets with files that had yet to be digitized, with the evidence room shoved into the back right corner. Though it looked like someone had gotten the blood out of the industrial carpet recently. Courteously put there by said deputy who'd turned out to be working for the cartel. Jocelyn tracked the chief around one of two desks and moved to set the plate on the end. "Have you had any luck finding a replacement deputy yet?"

Frustration tightened the fine lines etched around those incredibly dark eyes. "What do you want, Ms. Carville? Why are you really here?"

"I told you—I brought you cookies." She latched on to Maverick's collar as he tried to rush forward toward the treats.

"Nobody just brings cookies." Baker locked his sidearm in a drawer at the opposite end of the desk. "Not without wanting something in return, and certainly not when that someone is attached to one of the most dangerous and unrestricted security companies in the world."

And there it was. Him lumping her in with her employer. Seemed every time she managed to get a word in edgewise, Baker couldn't separate her from what she did for a living.

"I don't want anything in return." She motioned to the cookies she'd stayed up all night to bake. For him. Maverick was pawing at the carpet now, trying to get free. "I just thought you could use a little pick-me-up after everything that went down a couple weeks ago. I wanted to say—"

"A pick-me-up?" His dismissal hit harder than she'd expected. Baker faced her fully—a pure mountain of muscle built on secrets and defensiveness. He was a protector at heart, though. Someone who cared deeply about the people of this town. A man who believed in justice and righting wrongs. He had to be to do this kind of job day in and day out. "Let me make one thing clear, Ms. Carville. I'm not your friend. I don't want to pet your dog. I don't want you to bring me cookies or make arrangements for you to check on me to make sure I'm doing okay. You and I and that company you work for aren't allies. We won't be partnering on cases or braiding each other's hair. Police solve crimes. All you mercenaries do is make things worse in my town."

Mercenaries. Her heart threatened to shove straight up into her throat. That…that wasn't what she was at all. She helped people. She was the one who'd gotten Fire and Rescue in from surrounding towns when Sangre por Sangre had ambushed Alpine Valley and burned nearly a half dozen homes out of spite. She didn't hurt people for money, but no amount of explanation would change the chief's mind. He'd already created his own definition of her, and any fantasy she'd had that the two of them could work together or even become acquaintances instantly vanished.

Jocelyn's mouth dried as her courage to articulate any of that faltered. She almost reached for the cookies but thought better of it. "For your information, Maverick doesn't let anyone pet him. Not even me."

She dragged the K-9 with her and headed for the door, but Maverick ripped free of her hold. He sprinted toward the chief's desk. Embarrassment heated through her. Really? Of everything she could've left as her last words, it had to be about the fact her K-9 wasn't the cuddly type? And now Maverick was going to make her chase him. Great. No wonder she'd never won any argument about the importance of bonding as a team back at headquarters. She let herself be railroaded in the smallest conversations. No. She squared her shoulders. She wasn't going to let one tiff get the best of her. She was better than that, had overcome more than that.

But Maverick didn't go for the cookies.

Instead, he raced toward a door at the back and started sniffing at the carpet. The evidence room. Crap on a cracker. She didn't need this right now.

"You forgot your dog." The dismissiveness in Baker's tone told her he hadn't even bothered to look up to watch her leave.

"Thank you for your astute observation, Chief." Jocelyn dropped her hold on the front door. She'd almost made it out of there with her dignity in one piece. But it seemed that wasn't going to happen. At least not today. "You wouldn't happen to have any bomb tech in your evidence room, would you?"

Maverick's abilities to sniff out specific combinations of chemicals in explosives was unrivaled in his work as tactical-explosive-detection dog for the Department of Defense. And here in New Mexico. As cartels had battled over territory and attempted to upend law enforcement and local government, organizations like Sangre por Sangre had started planting devices where no one would find them—until it was too late. Soccer balls at parks, in a woman's purse at a restaurant in Albuquerque, a resident's home here in Alpine Valley. No one was safe. And so Socorro Security had recruited K-9s like Maverick onto the team in the name of strategy—find the threat before the threat found them. They were good at it, too. Protecting those who couldn't protect themselves. Ready to assist police and the DEA at a moment's notice. Founded by a former FBI investigator, Socorro had become the premier security company in the country by recruiting the best of the best. Former military operatives, strategists, combat specialists. They went above and beyond to take on this fight with the cartels. And they were winning.

Frustration and perhaps a hint of disbelief had Baker setting down his clipboard and pen on the desk. Closing the distance between them, the chief pulled his keys from his slacks once again. "Not that I know of. I can't account for every case, but most of what we keep here is from within the past five years. Unregistered arms, a few kilos. Maybe Fido smells the cheese I left in the rat trap last week."

Moving past her, Baker unlocked the door, shoving it open.

"He's a bomb-sniffing dog, Chief, and his name isn't Fido." She barely caught Maverick by the collar as he attempted to rush inside the small, overpacked room. The fluorescent tube light overhead flickered to life and highlighted rows and rows of labeled boxes in uniform shape and size.

A low beeping reached her ears.

Pivoting, Jocelyn set sights on the station's alarm panel near the front door—though it'd been disarmed when Baker had come inside a few minutes ago. "Do you hear that?"

Maverick pressed his face between two boxes on the lowest shelf and yipped. Her skin tightened in alarm.

"We have to get out of the building." Jocelyn un-pocketed her cell from her cargo pants and whistled low for Maverick to follow her out. The K-9 growled low to argue, but he'd obey. He *always* obeyed when it counted. She hit Ivy Bardot's contact information and raised the phone to her ear. Someone had planted a device in the police station. She needed full response.

"What?" Baker asked. "I can't just leave, Carville. In case you weren't aware, I'm the only officer on shift today."

They didn't have time for bickering. She grabbed on to his uniform collar and rushed to the front of the station with the chief in tow. "We have to go!"

Fire and sharp debris exploded across her back.

Jocelyn slammed into the nearest wall.

The world went dark.

HE SHOULD'VE GOTTEN out of the damn trailer.

Baker tried to get his legs underneath him, but the blast had ripped some crucial muscle he hadn't known had existed. Oh, hell. The wood paneling he'd surrounded himself day in and day out warbled in his vision. That wasn't good.

The explosion… It'd been a bomb. She'd tried to warn him. *Jocelyn.* Jocelyn Carville.

He shoved onto all fours. "Talk to me, Carville."

No answer.

Heat licked at his right shoulder as he tried to get himself oriented, but there was nothing for his brain to latch on to. The trailer didn't look the same as it had a few minutes ago. Nothing was where it was supposed to be, and now daylight was prodding inside from the corner where the evidence room used to be. Flames climbed the walls, eating up all that faux wood paneling and industrial carpet inch by inch. A weak alarm rang low in his ears. Maybe from next door?

They had to get out of here. "Jocelyn."

A whine pierced through the crackle of flames. He could just make out a distant siren through the opening that hadn't been there before the explosion. Fire and Rescue was on the way. But that wasn't the sound he'd heard. No, it'd been something sullen and hurt.

"Come on." His personalized pep talk wasn't doing any good. Baker shoved to stand, though not as balanced as he'd hoped. His hand nearly went through the trailer wall as he grasped for support. Smoke collected at the back of his throat. He stumbled forward. "Where the hell are you?"

Another whine punctured through the ringing in his head, and he waved off a good amount of black smoke to make out the outline ahead. The dog. Baker couldn't remember his name. The German shepherd was circling something on the floor. "Damn it."

He lunged for Jocelyn. She wasn't responding. Possibly injured. Moving her might make matters

worse, but the walls were literally closing in on them.
He'd have to drag her out. The shepherd had bitten on
to the shoulder of her Kevlar vest and was attempt-
ing to pull his handler to safety. Baker reached out.

The K-9 turned all that desperation onto Baker
with a warning and bared teeth. His ears darted
straight up, and suddenly he wasn't the bomb-
sniffing dog who'd tried to warn them of danger.
He was in protective mode. And he'd do anything
to keep Baker from hurting Jocelyn.

"Knock it off, Cujo. I'm trying to help." Baker
raised his hands, palms out, but no amount of deep
breathing was going to bring his heart rate down.
His mind went straight to the drawer where he'd
locked away his gun. He didn't want to have to put
the dog down, but if it came to getting Jocelyn out of
here alive or fighting off her pet, he'd have no other
choice. Though where the desk had gone, he couldn't
even begin to guess in this mess.

He leaned forward, moving slower than he wanted.
The fire was drawing closer. Every minute he wasted
trying to appease some guard dog was another minute Jocelyn might not have. Baker latched on to her
vest at both shoulders and pulled, waiting for the
shepherd to strike. "I'm here to help. Okay?"

The K-9 seemed to realize Baker wasn't going
to hurt its handler and softened around the mouth
and eyes.

"Good boy. Now let's get the hell out of here." He
hauled Jocelyn through a maze of debris and broken
glass out what used to be the front door. His body

ached to hell and back, but adrenaline was quickly drowning out the pain. Hugging her around the middle, he got her down the stairs with the German shepherd on her heels.

High-pitched sirens peeled through the empty park across the cul-de-sac and echoed off the surrounding cliffs protecting Alpine Valley. A lot of good they'd done these past few weeks. First a raid in which the cartel had burned down half a dozen homes. Now this.

Baker laid the woman in his arms across the old broken asphalt, shaded by her SUV. Ash darkened the distinct angles of her face, but it was the blood coming from her hairline that claimed the attention of every cell in his body. "Come on, Carville. Open your eyes."

Apparently she only took orders from her employer.

But she was breathing. That had to be enough for now—because there were still a whole lot of people in the trailer next door.

Baker set his sights on Fido. Bomb-sniffing dogs took commands, but he didn't have a clue how to order this one around. He pointed down at the K-9. "Uh, guard?"

Carville's sidekick licked his lips, cocking his head to one side.

"Stay." That had to be one. Baker swallowed the charred taste in his throat as he took in the remains of the station. Loss threatened to consume him as the past rushed to meet the present. No. He had to stay focused, get everyone out.

Fire and Rescue rounded the engine in front of what used to be the station as court staff escaped into the parking lot. Baker rushed to the other half of the trailer. A woman doubled over, nearly coughing up a lung.

He ran straight for her. "Is anyone still in there?"

She turned in a wild search. "Jason, our clerk! I don't see him!"

Baker hauled himself up the stairs, feeling the impact of the explosion with every step. Smoke consumed him once inside. It tendriled in random patterns as he waved one hand in front of his face but refused to disperse. Damn it. He couldn't see anything in here. "Hello! Jason? Are you still in here?"

Movement registered from his left. He tried to navigate through the cloud, fighting for his next breath, and hit the corner of a desk. The smoke must've been feeding in through the HVAC system, and without a giant hole in the ceiling it had nowhere to go. Smoke drove into his lungs. Burned. Baker tried to cough it up, but every breath was like inhaling fire. "Jason, can you hear me?"

He dared another few steps and hit something soft. Not another desk—too low. Sweat beaded down the back of his neck as a tile dropped from the ceiling. It shattered on the corner of another desk a couple feet away.

This place wasn't going to hold much longer. It was falling apart at the seams.

Reaching down, Baker felt a suit jacket with an arm inside and clamped onto it. "Sorry about the rug burn, man, but we gotta go."

Morning sunlight streaming through the glass door at the front of the trailer was the only map he had, but as soon as his brain had homed in on that small glimpse of hope, it was gone. The smoke closed in, suffocating him with every gasp for oxygen. Pin-pricks started in his fingers and toes. His body was starved for air. Soon he'd pass out altogether.

A flood of dizziness gripped tight, and he side-stepped to keep himself upright. "Not yet, damn it."

He wasn't going to pass out. Not now.

Baker forced himself forward. One step. Then another. His lungs spasmed for clean air, but there was no way to see if he was heading in the right di-rection. He just had to do the one thing that never ended well. He had to trust himself.

Seconds distorted into full minutes...into an hour...as he tried to navigate through the smoke. He was losing his grip on the court clerk. His legs finally gave into the percussion of the explosion. He dropped harder than a bag of rocks. The trailer floor shook beneath him. Black webs encroached on his vision. This was it. This was when the past finally claimed him.

Baker clawed toward where he thought the front door might be. Out of air. Out of fight. Hell, maybe he should've had one of those cranberry-lemon cook-ies as a last meal.

"Jocelyn."

He had no reason to settle on her name. They weren't friends. They weren't even acquaintances. If anything, they were on two separate sides of the war taking over this town. But over the past couple of months, caught in his darkest moments, she'd somehow provided a light when he'd needed it the most. With baked goods and smiles as bright as noon day sun.

The smoke cleared ahead.

A flood of sunlight cut through the blackness swallowing him whole.

"Chief Halsey!" Her voice cut through the haze eating up the cells in his brain, though it was more distorted than he was used to. Her outline solidified in front of him. Soft hands stretched an oxygen mask over his mouth and nose. "Don't worry. We're going to get you out of here."

A steady stream of fresh air fought back the sickness in his lungs, and he realized it wasn't Jocelyn's voice that time. It was deeper. Distinctly male. Another outline maneuvered past him and took to prying his grip from the court clerk. Baker let them. He clawed up the firefighter's frame and dragged himself outside with minimal help. It was amazing what oxygen could do to a starving body.

The sun pierced his vision and laid out a group of onlookers behind the century-old wood fence blocking off the station from the parking lot. A series of growls triggered his flight instinct, but Baker pushed away from the firefighter, keeping him on his feet. The dog. He'd ordered him to guard his handler.

Baker caught sight of the German shepherd from

the back of Alpine Valley's only Animal Control truck. Fido was trying to chew his way through the thin grate keeping him from his partner. Baker's instincts shot into high alert as he homed in on the unconscious woman on the ground, surrounded on either side by two EMS techs. He took a step forward. "Jocelyn?"

They'd stripped her free of her Kevlar vest to administer chest compressions—and exposed a bloodred stain spreading right in front of his eyes. He didn't understand. She'd been breathing when he'd left her.

Baker took a step forward. "What's happening? What's wrong with her?"

"Chief, we need you to keep your distance," one of the techs said. Though he couldn't be sure which one. "She's not responding. We need to get her in the bus. Now."

Strong hands forced him out of the way, but all he had attention for was Jocelyn, a mercenary he hadn't wanted anything to do with but who had insisted on sabotaging his life. Baker tried to follow, but the firefighter at his back was strong-arming him to stay at the scene. Helplessness surged as potent as that day he'd watched everything he'd built burn to the ground, and he wanted to fix it. To fix *this*. "Tell me what's happening."

But there was no time to answer.

The EMTs loaded Jocelyn onto a stretcher and raced for the ambulance. "Let's go! We're losing her!"

Chapter Two

Okay. Maybe cookies didn't make everything better.

Though she'd kill for one right now.

Jocelyn swallowed through the bitterness collecting at the back of her tongue, like she'd eaten something burned beyond recognition. And a grating rhythm wouldn't let up from one side. Ugh. She'd always hated that sound. As helpful as heart monitors were to let physicians and nurses know the patient was still alive, they could've set the damn sound on something far more pleasant.

That wasn't really what she was mad about, but it helped her focus. She curled her fingers into her palms. Her skin felt too tight. Dry. One look at the backs of her hands confirmed the blisters there. The monitor followed the spike in her heart rate, but the pain never came. That was the beauty of painkillers. They masked the hurt inside. But only temporarily. Sooner or later, she'd have to face it. Though, based on the slow drip into her IV, she still had some time.

"Here I thought a visit from Socorro would be the worst part of my day." Recognition flared hot and uncomfortable as Chief Baker Halsey leaned forward in the chair set beside her bed. A few scratches marred that otherwise flawless face she'd memorized over the past six months. It was easy, really. To catch herself watching him. To lose herself in that quiet intensity he exuded. "Sorry to tell you I couldn't save the cookies."

"Good thing I made extra." She tried to sit up in the bed, but the mattress was too soft. It threatened to swallow her whole if she wasn't careful. Glaring white tile and cream-washed walls closed in around her. Right back where she didn't want to be. Her attention shifted to the chart at the end of her bed. Her medical history would be in there. Clear for all physicians and nurses to see. What she could and couldn't have in moments like this. A wave of self-consciousness flared behind her rib cage. Would the hospital keep it confidential during the investigation into the bombing? Or did Baker already know? "You got me out?"

"You wanted me to leave you there?" He was distracting himself again, looking anywhere but at her. "It was nothing. If it hadn't been for that small moose you order around, I would've gotten you out quicker. Maybe realized you'd taken a piece of shrapnel sooner."

Maverick. Her nerves went under attack. If he'd been hurt in the blast… Fractured memories of the seconds leading up to the explosion frayed the harder she tried to latch on to them. The monitor on the other side of the bed went wild. "Where is he?"

"Animal Control got hold of him at the scene. He was trying to fight off the EMTs, but that might've been my fault." Baker spread his hands in a wide gesture, highlighting the scraps and bruising along his forearms. "I told him to guard you before I nearly died trying to get a clerk out of the other side of the trailer. Apparently Fido took me seriously."

She didn't have the energy to fight back about Maverick's name. "But he's okay? He's not hurt?"

"Yeah. He's fine." Confusion, tainted with a hint of concern, etched deep into Baker's expression. "Gotta tell you, Carville. I figured you'd be more worried about the chunk of metal they had to take out of you than your sidekick."

"Maverick saved our lives." It was all she was willing to offer right then. "If it wasn't for him picking up that bomb, neither of us would've made it out of that trailer."

"You're right. I'm sorry." Baker scrubbed one busted up hand down his face, and suddenly it was as though he'd aged at least three years. He looked heavy and exhausted and beaten. Same as when he'd discovered one of his own deputies had secretly been working for the cartel.

Her chest constricted at witnessing the pain he carried, but she couldn't focus on that right now. They had more important things to contend with. Like the fact that Alpine Valley's police department was under attack. "Any leads?"

"Nothing yet. Albuquerque's bomb squad is en route. As of right now, all I've got is theories." Baker leaned back in his seat. "Alpine Valley hasn't seen any bombings like this before. Most of what we respond to is domestic calls and overdoses."

Until recently. He didn't have to say the words—the implication was already there. A fraction of residents in Alpine Valley had rallied against a military contractor setting up their headquarters so close to town. They'd believed having the federal government so close would aggravate relations between Sangre por Sangre and the towns at their mercy. So far, they'd been right.

"Socorro employs a combat controller," Jocelyn said. "Jones Driscoll has investigated IEDs overseas. I'm sure he'd be able to help until the bomb squad can get here."

"You want me to bring in a mercenary to investigate the bombing." It wasn't a question.

She wasn't sure if it was the pain medication, his determination to call her K-9 by the wrong name or his insistence that she was part of a group of people who killed targets for money. None of it was sitting very well with the explosive memories fighting for release and the blisters along the backs of her hands. Her determination to hang on to the silver lining was slipping, threatening to put her right back into the hole she'd spent months crawling out of. "Is that all you think of me when you see me in town? When I handed you that piece of lemon bread or brought you those cookies earlier today? Do you really look at me and see a killer?"

He didn't answer.

"Either you just don't get it or you don't want to—I don't know which, and frankly, I don't really care—but you and I are on the same team. We want the same thing. To keep Sangre por Sangre from claiming Alpine Valley and all those other towns just like it." She didn't like this. Being the one to tell the hard truths. Dipping her toes in that inky-black pool of who she used to be. "Socorro has federal resources you'll never be able to get your hands on, and shutting us out will be the worst thing you can do for the people you claim to be protecting. So use us. Use *me*."

Tension flexed the muscles running from his neck and along his shoulders as he straightened in the chair. Such a minor movement, but one that spoke volumes. The small fluctuations in that guarded expression released. "Does the dog have to come with the deal?"

The knot in her stomach relaxed a bit. Not entirely, but enough she could take a full breath. After months of pushing back, Baker was entertaining the thought of trusting someone outside of his small circle of officers. It was a step in the right direction. "Yeah. He does."

"All right, but I'm not going to blindly trust a bunch of mercs—*soldiers*—without getting the lay of the land first. I want to meet your team." A defensiveness she'd always wanted to work beyond encapsulated him back into chief mode, where no one could get through. "This is still my investigation. I make the calls. Everything pertaining to this case comes through me. I want background checks, service records, financials, right down to what you're all allergic to—the whole enchilada. Understand?"

Mmm. Enchiladas. Okay. Maybe a half a roll of cookie dough for breakfast wasn't the best idea she'd had today.

"I think that can be arranged." Jocelyn felt the inner warmth coming back, the darkness retreating. This was how it was supposed to be. Her and Baker working together for a common goal in the name of justice. Not on opposite sides of the table. Still, as hard as she might try to keep sunshine and unicorns throughout her days, she wasn't going to roll over to the chief's every whim. "But I have a condition of my own. You have to call Maverick by his real name."

A small break in that composure sent victory charging through the aching places in her body. "Why does that matter? It's not like he's going to take orders from me. I already tried that. Look how it turned out—he almost took my hand off."

"Maverick is very protective when he needs to be, but he deserves your respect after saving your life back at the station," she said.

"All right, then. Maverick. Easy to remember. He's not going to growl at me every time I'm around, is he?" Baker looked around the room as though expecting her K-9 partner to appear out of thin air.

"He just needs a couple minutes to get to know you. Maybe take in a good crotch sniffing." She tried to keep her smile under control, but the outright terror contorting Baker's face was too much. *This.* She'd missed this. The bickering, the smiles and private jokes. She hadn't gotten to experience it in a long time. Not since before her last tour. "I'm kidding."

Baker's exhale outclassed a category-one tornado. The tightness around his eyes smoothed after a few seconds. Wow. The man acted as though he'd never heard a joke before. This was going to be fun. "Oh. Good. In that case, I'm not really sure what we're supposed to do now."

"I think this is the part where you hike down to the cafeteria and get me one of those enchiladas you were just talking about. You know, seeing as how I'm injured and you're…" She motioned to the entire length of him. "Just sitting there with barely a scratch."

"You haven't seen the inside of my lungs."

A mere crack of his smile twisted her stomach into knots. Well, look at that. It did exist.

Baker pushed to stand, in all his glory. "I thought all you Socorro types ran on nuclear power. Never stopped or slowed down for anything when you took on an assignment. You're like that weird pink bunny with the drum."

"You're thinking of Cash Meyers, our forward scout, when he took on the cartel a few weeks ago." Made a hell of a mess in the process. Destroying Sangre por Sangre headquarters in an effort to recover a woman who'd become the obsession of a cartel lieutenant. His personal mission had been a success, too. Cash had brought the entire organization to its knees for the woman he loved.

A flare of pain bit into her heart at the memory

of what that felt like. Of not being able to save the people you cared about the most.

Nervous energy shot through her. She couldn't just sit here. That gave the bad feelings permission to claw out of the box she'd shoved them into at the back of her mind.

Jocelyn threw off the covers, only acutely aware of the open-backed gown she'd been forced into upon admittance. She grabbed for her singed pants and slid them on with as much dignity as she could muster. Which wasn't much given she was still attached to the damn monitors. "I happen to run on powdered sugar, a whole lot of butter and melted cheese."

Baker handed off her jacket as she pulled the nodes from her skin. Such a simple gesture. But one that wasn't coated in sarcasm or negativity. Progress. "Not sure anyone has ever told you this, but your idea of an enchilada sounds disgusting."

WHAT THE HELL had he been thinking agreeing to this?

Baker notched his head back to take in the height of the building as Jocelyn pulled into the underground parking garage. Sleek, modern angles, black reflective windows—the place was like something out of an old spy movie. Half-built into the canyon wall behind it, Socorro Security headquarters swallowed them whole. He was in the belly of the beast now. Who knew if he'd ever make it out.

Jocelyn navigated through the garage as though she'd done it a thousand times before. Which made sense. As far as he could tell, she, like the rest of her team lived, worked, ate and slept out of this building. No visitors as far as he'd been able to discern in his spurts of surveillance. If the operators employed here had personal lives, he hadn't seen a lick of it, and Baker couldn't help but wonder about the woman in the driver's seat as she shoved the SUV into Park.

She took out what looked like a black credit card. Heavy, too. Aluminum, if he had to guess. Maybe an access card. The bandages wrapping the blisters along the backs of her hands and wrists brightened under limited lighting coming through the windshield.

"I get one of those?" he asked.

She shook her head. "I didn't think accessing the elevators was high on your priority list of things to do today. Otherwise I would've had one made in your honor."

"What? No access to the secret vault?" He watched her pocket the card.

"Sorry. That's reserved for VIP members." Her laugh burned through him with surprising force as she climbed out of the vehicle. The flimsy fabric the hospital staff claimed was an actual piece of clothing was gone. She'd somehow managed to get herself dressed without much distress. Guess that was the upside of painkillers after getting stitched up.

While the EMTs had been forced to remove her Kevlar vest to get access to her wound, it seemed she carried an extra. As though she expected an ambush at any moment. In fact, Baker couldn't think of a time when she didn't have that added layer of protection. Even at the Christmas bake sale.

"You'll have to pay extra for that tour," she said.

He followed close on her heels, absorbing everything about the parking lot he could with barely visible lighting and cement walls. Most likely designed that way to confuse anyone stupid enough to try to breach this place. Though Jocelyn seemed to know exactly where she was going. Still, collecting as much information on these people as he could get would only prove his theory about military contractors' lack of interest in protecting towns like Alpine Valley.

"You been with Socorro long?"

She pressed the key card to a smooth section of wall off to her left and stepped back. "Six months. Signed on a little after my last tour."

Elevator doors parted to reveal a silver car.

Jocelyn stepped inside, holding the door open for him as he boarded.

His limited knowledge of gender representation in the military filtered through the catalogue he was building on her in his head. "Air Force?"

"Army." The small muscles in her jaw flexed under pressure. "Logistics coordinator. Same job I do for Socorro."

Baker filed that away for future reference. Logistics coordinators weren't just responsible for keeping track of military assets. They procured rare resources in times of panic, stayed on top of maintenance operations and covered transportation of any materials, facilities and personnel. People in her position were essential to strategy and planning in the middle of war zones and conflicts. Without operatives like her, the entire military would grind to a halt.

He noted which pocket she slid her key card into despite the admiration cutting through him. "Deployed overseas?"

"Afghanistan. Two tours. Then a third in Africa." There was something missing in that statement. It took him longer than it should have to recognize it, but no one else in his life had the ridiculous positivity Jocelyn seemed to emanate with every word out of her mouth. She didn't like talking about her service in the military. Interesting.

"Wow. Right in the middle of the action." He'd known a couple of deputies from surrounding towns who'd served in the Middle East over the past decade. None of them had held a candle to Jocelyn's level of optimism after what they'd seen. Question was: Was it just for show or a genuine part of her personality? Hard to tell.

The doors parted, dropping them off in the middle of the freaking Death Star. Gleaming black walls with matching tile. The artwork nearly blended in with the walls, only distinguished by outline of the frames. Blinding fluorescent lights reflected off the floors like a crazy hall of mirrors as Jocelyn led them through what he thought might be a hallway.

"Everybody's waiting for us in the conference room," she said.

He tried to map out a mental route through the maze, but there was just too much to index. Everything looked the same. How the hell did anyone navigate this place? "You have many visitors come through here?"

"No. Just you." She wrenched open a glass double door and held it open for him. Not an ounce of pain from her wound reflected in her expression. Hell, just thinking about his body slamming into the trailer wall made him want to cry. How did she do that? Jocelyn motioned him inside. "Welcome to the inner circle."

A wall-to-ceiling window—bulletproof, if he had to guess—stretched along the backside of the conference room. The oversized table led to two Socorro representatives waiting for their arrival. One he recognized. Driscoll. Jones Driscoll. He was the company's head of combat operations, according to Jocelyn. Someone who could help them with the investigation into the bombing. Made sense he'd be here. But the other... Baker didn't know her.

"Chief Halsey, thank you for joining us. I'm Ivy Bardot." The redhead stood from her seat at the head of the table, smoothing invisible wrinkles from her black slacks.

This was the founder of Socorro Security. Jocelyn's boss. Taller than he'd expected, thin and pale, with a few freckles dotted across the bridge of her nose. He hadn't been able to gather much intel on her other than a minuscule peek at her federal record. Former FBI. Highest number of cases closed in Bureau history, which meant she had to be damn good at her job. But clearly...unfulfilled. Why else would she have started Socorro and dragged a team out into the middle of the desert? Emerald-green eyes assessed him as easily as he'd assessed her, but Baker wasn't going to let her get into his head.

Ivy extended her hand. "I'm glad we finally have a chance to meet."

He took her hand out of social obligation as he tracked Jocelyn around the table before she took her seat down by Driscoll. "Yeah, well. Keep the enemy close and all that."

"Is that what we are?" Ivy withdrew her hand, careful not to let those perfectly manicured eyebrows move a millimeter. She was good. Maybe as good as he was at keeping other people in the dark. No, probably better.

In truth, he didn't know what they were at the moment. Not partners, that was for damn sure. Because the minute he trusted these people, they'd leave him and Alpine Valley for dead. They were a temporary solution. One at the mercy of the feds with no real attachment to his town.

"I've got a bombing investigation to get back to, so let's skip the small talk and get this over with," he said.

"A man after my own heart. Please, sit." Ivy headed back to her seat at the head of the table—a position of power she obviously cared about. "This is Jones Driscoll, head of our combat unit. He's our expert in all explosive ordinance and IEDs."

Baker nodded a greeting at the bearded, tattooed mountain man who looked like he belonged in the middle of a logging site rather than in a sleek conference room. Then took a seat beside Jocelyn. He interlocked his hands together over the surface of the table, right beside hers. "Albuquerque bomb squad got to the scene a couple hours ago. They're still trying to put the device back together, but from what little I saw of it before the explosion, we're most likely looking at homemade. Given your experience, I'm not sure why you'd want to attach yourself to a random bombing case."

"Because I don't believe this is random, Chief." Driscoll cut his attention to the company's founder, who nodded in turn. The combat head pried open a folder Baker hadn't noticed until then. "I took the liberty of getting in touch with Albuquerque's squad. They forwarded photos taken of what's left of the station."

"You went over my head." He barely had a second to give in to the annoyance clawing through him.

Driscoll templed his fingers over one of the photos from the stack and spun it around to share with the others. "The device that exploded in your station this morning? I've seen it before. In a car bombing outside of Ponderosa three months ago. The truck belonged to the chief of police there. Andrew Trevino."

Ponderosa. Baker sat a bit straighter under the weight of Jocelyn's gaze as he tried to come to terms with this new information. None of this made sense. He reached for the photos. "I haven't heard about any car bombing."

"You wouldn't have. Socorro was called to the

scene. Ponderosa PD kept as much as they could from the media out of respect for their chief," Ivy said.

"What the hell does that mean?" He locked his gaze on each of the operators in turn, but none of them were giving him an answer.

"It's not uncommon for the cartel to target law enforcement officers it believes might intercept their plans or to make an example out of them in front of the towns they want to move in on." Driscoll tapped his index finger onto the photo positioned between them. "It shows control. Power. Manipulation. Call it your friendly cartel calling card."

"You're saying this was a targeted attack." Baker sifted through the possible scenarios in a matter of seconds. He'd taken this job to keep what had happened to him from happening to anyone else, but most of the cases he'd tackled since being elected to chief hadn't invited this type of attack. Who the hell would want to kill him? "The bomb was left for me."

Chapter Three

She could be miserable before she had a cookie and miserable after she had a cookie, but she could never be miserable while she was eating one. Or the dough.

Jocelyn dug out another spoonful from the Tupperware container in which she'd saved the last bit of cranberry-lemon dough. Whoever had said raw cookie dough would make her sick was a liar. Some of the best memories she had were between her and a bowl of homemade dough. Though some kinds whisked away the pain better than others. Gauging the mental list of ingredients she'd need, she calculated how fast she could whip up some chocolate chip dough while Baker was floating every other theory past Jones other than the most obvious.

Someone had planted a bomb in his station. Timed it well enough to ensure Baker would be in the trailer. And then detonated it with him inside. Well, they couldn't actually be sure of that last theory until the Albuquerque bomb squad recovered all the bits and pieces of the device. But how many other options were there?

Heavy footsteps registered, breaking her out of her thoughts. One of the most dangerous places to be. Cash Meyers—Socorro's forward observer—angled into the kitchen, dusted with red dirt. He'd been in town again, helping rebuild the homes Sangre por Sangre had destroyed in their last raid. She could see it in the bits of sawdust on his shoulder.

He nodded at her in the way most of the men on the team did, his chin hiking slightly upward. "Heard you saw some fireworks this morning."

"Quite the show, for sure." Her phone vibrated from the inside of her cargo pants, but she wasn't ready to leave the protective walls of the kitchen. To acknowledge there was an entire world out there. This was where she thrived. Where nothing existed past the buzz of her stand mixer, the radiant heat of the oven and timers beeping in her ears. Jocelyn stuck the end of her spoon through the softening combination of butter, flour, sugar and cranberries. "Got a souvenir, too. Unfortunately, they made me hand it over to the bomb squad. Otherwise I'd put it on my bookshelf."

"You're sick, Carville." Cash wrenched the refrigerator open and grabbed a bottle of water. In less than thirty seconds, he downed the entire thing. Then he tossed the bottle into the recycling bin—her initiative—and leveled that remarkably open gaze on her. It was the little changes like that Jocelyn had noted over the past couple of months. Ever since Cash had taken up with his client. Elena. She'd done something to him. Made him as soft as this cookie dough to the point that he wasn't entirely annoying to be around. "You good?"

"I'm good." What other answer could she possibly give? That the pain in her side was the only thing keeping her from running back into the numbness she'd relied on before she'd come to Socorro? That the mere notion of painkillers threatened to drop her back into a vicious cycle that absolutely terrified her? Cash Meyers wasn't the person nor the solution she needed right then. Nobody on her team fit the bill. After loading her spoon into the dishwasher, she topped off the Tupperware and set it back in the fridge. "Tell Elena I'll drop off a batch tomorrow. I know she and Daniel really like my peanut butter cookies."

She moved past Cash and into the hallway. Air pressurized in her chest. It was always like this. Like she was preparing for war. Only in her case, the metaphor fit better than anything else. The onslaught of pain and suffering and death outside these bulletproof walls had the ability to crush her. It was a constant fight not to retreat, to hide, to fail those she'd sworn she would help. Even a grumpy chief of police.

"Jocelyn." Cash's use of her first name stopped her cold. The men and women of Socorro worked together as a team. They relied on one another to get them through their assignments and to keep each other alive. They were acquaintances with the same goal: dismantling the cartel. While most military units bonded through down time, inside jokes and pranks, the people she worked beside always managed to keep a bit of physical and emotional distance. Especially when addressing one another. The fact that Cash had resorted to verbally using her name meant only one thing. Her cover was slipping. "You sure you're all right?"

She pasted on that smile—the one honed over months of practice—and turned to face him. In an instant, the heaviness of the day drained from her overly tense muscles, and she was right back where she needed to be. "Never better. Stop worrying so much. You'll get crow's feet."

Jocelyn navigated along the black-on-black halls and faced off with the conference room door. Baker was still there, immobile in front of the window stretching from floor to ceiling as the sun dipped behind the mountains to the west. One arm crossed over his chest, the other scrubbing along his jawline. She catalogued every movement as though the slightest shift in his demeanor actually mattered. It didn't, but convincing her brain otherwise was a lost cause.

Stretching one hand out, she wrapped her fingers around the door handle. She could still feel the heat flaring up her hands as she'd tried to take the brunt of the explosion for him. It'd been reactive. Part of her job. Nothing more. At least, that was what she kept telling herself. The bandages across the backs of her hands started itching as she shoved through the door. "You're still here. Figured you and Jones would already be meeting up with the bomb squad back in town."

Turning toward her, Baker dropped his hands to

his sides. Desert sunlight cut through the corner of the window at his back and cast him in blinding light. It highlighted the bruises along one side of his face. A small cut at his temple, too. "Guess he had something else to take care of. Said I could wait for you here."

"Right. Makes sense you would need a ride back into town." She tried not to take it personally. Of all the operators Socorro employed, her skill set didn't do much good in a bombing investigation.

"Well, yes. And no." Nervous energy replaced the mask Baker usually wore. "He told me you were the first one who responded to that car bombing in Ponderosa. Thought maybe you could walk me through it, see if anything lines up with what happened at the station."

"You mean other than the fact that the bomb that went off this morning wasn't attached to the undercarriage of your car?" she asked.

"Right." His low-key laugh did something funny to her insides.

As though she'd subconsciously been holding her breath just to hear it. Which was ridiculous. He didn't want to be here. Baker didn't want her help. He wanted to solve the case. She was only a means to an end. Tendrils of hollowness spread through her chest. Exhaustion was winning out after surviving the impact of the explosion. Her hand went to her side for Maverick but met nothing but empty air. Right. Animal Control.

"You know you won't be able to go back to your

place," she said. "At least not until we have a better idea behind the bomber's motive. Too risky."

"I've been crashing on the couch at the station for a while." Baker rounded the head of the conference table, closing the distance between them. A lungful of smoke burned the back of her throat. Still dressed in his uniform, he was walking around smelling as though he'd just stepped out of one of those joints that smoked their meat instead of barbecuing it. Her stomach rumbled at the sensory overload. "Does that make me homeless?"

"Well, it certainly doesn't make you stable." Her instinct to take on the problems of the people around her—a distraction she'd come to rely on through the hard times—flared hot, but Baker wasn't the kind to share. Let alone trust a mercenary with personal information. She could help, though. Maybe that would ease the tightness in her stomach.

Jocelyn headed for the conference room door. "Come on. I'm sure one of the guys has something you can wear. You can borrow my shower while I find us something to eat."

"Why are you doing this?" His voice barely carried to her position at the door, but every cell in her body amplified it as though he'd spoken into a megaphone. "Why are you helping me?"

"Because despite what you might think of Socorro, Chief, helping people is what we do." She didn't want to think about the ones she hadn't been able to save. The ones who took up so much space in her heart. "It's why we all enlisted. Whether it be military or law enforcement. It's what keeps us going. It might not seem like much, but even the slightest deviation from a recipe can alter the taste of a dessert. It makes a difference."

"Damn it. I was hoping you were going to say something like money or authority or to take credit for dismantling the cartel." His expression softened. "And now I'm hungry."

"Sorry to disappoint you." The bruising along one shoulder barked as she hauled the heavy glass door inward, but she'd live. Thanks to him. "We've got some prepackaged meals in the kitchen. I'll grab you one while you clean up."

"Baker," he said from behind.

She hadn't made it more than two steps before the significance of his name settled at the base of her spine. "What?"

"We survived a bombing together, and you and your employer are going out of their way to help me find who did it." He slipped busted knuckles into his uniform slack pockets, taking the intensity out of his body language. "You can call me Baker."

The chief was asking her to call him by his first name. Giving her permission to step beyond the professional boundaries he'd kept between them since the moment they'd met. It shouldn't have held so much weight, but in her line of work, the gravity hit as hard as that explosion.

"Baker." She could practically taste his name on her tongue. Mostly sour with a hint of sweetness. Like a lemon tart packed with sweet cream.

Or maybe she just needed to brush her teeth.

"This doesn't taste like an MRE." Baker stabbed his fork into another helping of turkey, mashed potatoes and green beans and took a bite. It was enough to thaw the past few hours of adrenaline loss and brought his blood sugar back in line.

"It's not." Sitting straight across the table from him, Jocelyn scooped up a forkful of what looked like chicken with some kind of green vegetable and brought it to her mouth. As she chewed, her hair slid over her one shoulder, brushing the surface of the table. Unremarkably mesmerizing. "I put together about six dozen meals every week to make sure we're not living off carbs and protein shakes."

He wasn't sure if it was the blast or finally getting something other than microwave noodles in his stomach, but Baker had only just noted the way the light reflected off the black waves of hair she usually kept in tight rein. A hint of sepia colored her skin from long days out in the desert, but there wasn't a single piece of evidence of sun damage. Jocelyn Carville fit the exact opposite of everything he'd expected of a soldier, yet there was no denying the part she played in helping him with this investigation. "You made this? Hell, maybe I need to come out here more often."

Jocelyn pressed the back of her hand to her mouth to keep her food in place. "I'd drop some off at the station, but as of this morning, I'm not really sure where I would take it. Have you heard anything from the Albuquerque bomb squad?"

Right. The station he'd taken to holing up in had become a crime scene. He'd almost forgotten about that, sitting here as though the world had stopped and nothing existed outside of this place. They'd taken their seats at an oversized dining table set just on the other side of the kitchen that didn't look as though it got much use. Though from what he knew of Socorro, the contractors had been here for over a year. Maybe they just didn't use the table due to the onslaught of assignments. "Not yet. It may be a few days, but once they have something solid, it's only a matter of time before we find the bomber."

All he needed was proof the bombing was tied to the cartel, and ATF would get involved. Then he could finally take down Sangre por Sangre. For good.

Baker forced himself to focus on his next bite and not the way Jocelyn's eyes practically lit up as she savored her meal. The woman liked food—that much he could tell. Lemon bread, cranberry cookies, full-sized meals packaged in to-go containers. Her physical training had to be hell to stay as lean as she did. Then again, he wasn't entirely sure what was under all that gear she insisted on carrying throughout the day. Even indoors. Then again, what the hell was he doing noticing anything about her when they had a case to work?

"Tell me what you remember of the bombing outside Ponderosa," he said.

"Sure." She hiked one knee into her chest. Playful. Relaxed. At home. The feeling almost bled across the table and seeped into his aching joints with its easiness. Almost. "Ponderosa PD called it in. They hadn't been able to get a hold of their chief that morning, even though he was scheduled for the first shift. The sergeant sent out two patrols. One of them came across the scene about a mile outside of town in one of the canyons nearby. Too far away for anyone to notice."

She took a sip of water. "It was a pickup truck matching the description of Chief Andrew Trevino's vehicle. They initially believed it'd been a fire. That maybe Trevino had forgotten to clean up some oil from under the hood or had a gas leak. He was a smoker. His deputies wanted to believe it'd been an accident."

"But you determined otherwise." Her combat teammate—Jones Driscoll—had said as much, and Baker couldn't help but wonder what an optimistic, high-spirited woman like Jocelyn had seen in her life to make that assessment.

Her gaze detached, as though she were seeing it all play out right in front of her. "The front half of the vehicle was missing. Not even a gasoline fire would instigate that kind of damage. I went through what was left behind, but the resulting fire had burned away most of the evidence. Except a police badge. The edges had melted slightly, but it was clear who was in the vehicle when the bomb discharged."

It was easy to picture. Her crouched in the dirt, studying a replica of the badge currently pinned to his chest. Would she have done the same thing had he been killed in today's bombing? Acid surged up his throat at the notion.

"Maverick recovered a piece of the device. It wasn't sophisticated in the least, but it got the job done. Jones was the one who determined nitroglycerin had been used as the explosive. He could smell it. Anyone with an internet connection can build a bomb, but there was one distinct piece of evidence we couldn't ignore that helped us determine it was planted by the cartel." Jocelyn twisted her fork into the center of her dish but didn't take another bite. "The pager used to trigger the device was registered to a shell company owned by one of Sangre por Sangre's lieutenants. Benito Ramon. Has a history of arson and a mass of other charges, growing up in the cartel."

Confirmation that his leads weren't dead after all sparked anticipation through his veins, but he ate another forkful of dinner to settle his nerves.

"I read about him." Baker wouldn't tell her why. "Sixteen bombings all over the state, each suspected of linking back to Sangre por Sangre, but there was never any evidence to prove he was the bomber. From what I understand the man is a ghost, a legend the cartel uses to keep towns like Alpine Valley in line. Like the boogie man."

Tingling pooled at the base of his spine. He'd never been able to find evidence Benito Ramon existed. All he'd uncovered was a trail of death and destruction when he'd assumed the mantle of chief of police. Crime scene photos, witness accounts, evidence logs—none of it had led to the man who'd taken everything Baker cared about. Until now.

"Ghosts—real or otherwise—can still do a lot of damage," she said.

He could almost read a hint of suspicion in her voice—as though he'd somehow become attuned to the slightest inflection since they'd survived the explosion together. "You think something else was going on. That's why Jones wants you involved in this investigation."

Her mouth parted. Jocelyn didn't answer for a series of seconds. Considering how much to tell him? Then again, he guessed that was the problem with military contractors. Always working their own agenda.

"You said it yourself," she said. "There was never any evidence Benito Ramon was responsible for those sixteen bombings. So why would he make the mistake of using a pager registered to one of his shell companies to trigger the bomb that killed Chief Trevino?"

Good question. Hell, one he should've had the sense to ask himself. "You think someone was trying to pin the chief's murder on Benito Ramon?"

"It's just a theory." Jocelyn collected her meal, snapped the storage lid on top and shoved to her feet. She set the food back in the refrigerator with far more grace than he'd expected out of a five-foot-five woman carrying at least thirty pounds of gear. There was a hidden strength in the way she moved. Practiced.

A theory. He could work with a theory. Baker gathered up his own dinner and set about disposing of what he couldn't finish. "This place is a lot quieter than I figured it'd be."

"Socorro is on call 24/7. It's hard to get everyone together when we're all working different shifts, but we try." An inner glow that hadn't been there a few minutes ago seeped into her expression. "Birthday parties, movie nights, Thanksgiving and Christmas. It's rare, but being together helps us bond better as a team, you know? Takes the harshness out of the work we do."

Baker watched the transformation right in front of him. Where a heaviness had tensed the muscles along her neck and shoulders, exhilaration took its place as she talked about her team. He'd never seen anything like it before. "You like this kind of stuff. Cooking, baking for people, movie nights…"

There was a hitch in Jocelyn's step that she tried to cover up as she moved from one side of the kitchen to the next. She'd taken a mixing bowl out of the refrigerator and peeled the plastic wrap free. Cookie dough, from the look of it. Did the woman ever just sit still? She dragged a cookie scoop out of one of the drawers and started rolling the dough into perfect golf ball–sized pieces onto a baking sheet. "Of course. Keeps me busy."

"Aren't you already busy responding to things like car bombings and coordinating resources from surrounding towns?" He couldn't help but watch her roll one section of dough before moving onto the next. It was a highly coordinated dance that seemed to have no end and drove his nervous system into a frenzy. He wanted to reach out, to force her hands to stop working, but Baker had the distinct impression she'd bite him if he interrupted. Like her dog almost had back at the station.

"Well, yeah, but this ends in cookies. And who doesn't like cookies?" Her smile split a small cut at one corner of her mouth. A sliver of blood peeked through.

His discipline failed him right then. Baker closed the short distance between them, swiping the blood from her mouth. One touch catapulted his heart rate into overdrive. A sizzle of heat burned across his skin faster than the flames created by the bomb this morning.

Instant paralysis seemed to flood through her. She stopped rolling dough into bite-sized balls, her hands buried deep in something that smelled a lot like peanut butter. Three seconds passed. Four. Her exhale brushed against the underside of his jaw.

Jocelyn took as big of a step back as she could with her palms full of dough. "What are you doing?"

"I'm sorry." He knew better than to touch her without permission. Cold infused his veins as he brushed his thumb against his slacks. They were already spotted with blood. A few more drops wouldn't hurt. "You just…had a bit of blood on you."

"Don't. Just…don't." Lean muscle running the length

of her arms flexed and receded as she peeled layers of dough off her hands and tossed it back into the bowl.

Right before she sprinted from the kitchen.

Chapter Four

No amount of cookie dough was going to fix this.

Jocelyn scrubbed her hands as hard as she could beneath the scalding water. She could still feel his touch at the corner of her mouth. Baker's touch. It'd been calloused and soft at the same time, depending on which feeling she wanted to focus on. Only problem was she didn't actually want to focus on any of it.

Her skin protested each swipe of the loofa. To the point it'd turned a bright red. The blisters she'd earned this morning were bleeding again, but it wasn't enough to make her stop. The dough just wouldn't come off. She could still feel it. Still feel Baker's thumb pressed against her skin.

"Jocelyn?" Movement registered in the mirror behind her. Baker centered himself over her shoulder though ensured to keep his distance. Dark circles embedded beneath his eyes, taking the defiance and intensity she was used to right out of him.

She ordered one hand to turn off the water, but she just kept scrubbing, trying to replace one feeling with another. It was working. Slowly. The tightness in her chest was letting go. "How did you get in here?"

"That guy Cash told me where your room was. I knocked, but there was no answer. I just wanted to make sure you were okay." His voice didn't hold the same authority it had while he'd been asking her about the bombing in Ponderosa.

"So you thought you would just let yourself in?" The conversation was helping, somehow easing her heart rate back into normal limits.

"I knocked for fifteen minutes," he said. "Listen… I'm sorry about before. I shouldn't have touched you. I was out of line, and it won't happen again. I give you my word."

Her hands were burning, and the last few pieces of agitation slipped free. She finally had enough control to turn off the water. All was right with the world. Jocelyn reached for the pretty hand towel to her left and took a solid full breath for the first time in minutes. "I'm not crazy."

Three distinguished lines between his eyebrows deepened as she caught his reflection in the mirror. "That didn't even cross my mind. A lot of soldiers have trouble differentiating the past trauma from the present. I've seen it in one of my deputies. There's no shame—"

"I'm not suffering from PTSD, Baker." She rearranged the hand towel back on its round metal hardware. No one understood. Because what she'd done—what she lived with every day—was hers alone. But what she wouldn't give to let someone else take the weight for a while.

Jocelyn turned to face him, the bathroom door-frame putting them on opposite sides of the divide. Here and outside these walls. "You want to know why I bake so many cookies and breads and cakes and pies? Why I feel safer with a glob of dough in my hands than with my sidearm? Because it makes me happy. It helps me forget."

"Forget what?" He moved toward her then, resurrecting that hint of smoke in his uniform.

Discomfort alienated the pleasure she'd found with her hands in that peanut butter dough. She'd already let her control slip once today. Did she really want to take a full dive into trusting a man who couldn't even stand to be in the same room as her? "My husband."

"Oh." His expression went smooth as he leaned against the doorjamb. "I didn't realize you're married."

"Was. I was married." She'd never said the words before, never wanted to admit there was this gaping hole inside of her where Miles used to be. Because that would be when the sadness got to be too much. When the world tore straight out from under her and past comforts reared their ugly little heads. "He passed away about a year ago."

"I'm sorry." Folding his arms over his chest, Baker looked as though he belonged. Not just here in headquarters but in this moment. "I didn't... I didn't know."

"Nobody knows. No one but you." She let her words fill the space between them, but the weight didn't get lighter. If anything, her legs threatened to collapse in the too-small bathroom attached to her room.

Eyes to the floor, Baker scrubbed a hand down his face. "So when I touched you—"

"It wasn't your fault." She crossed her feet in front of her, her weight leveraged against the vanity. Of all the places she'd imagined having this conversation, in a bathroom with the Alpine Valley's chief of police hadn't even made the list. "The most affection I get now days is from Maverick, and he's not as cuddly as he looks. You just…took me by surprise is all."

"As cuddly as he looks? Your dog nearly took my hand off when I was trying to get you out of the station."

His attempt to lighten the mood worked to a degree. But there was still a matter of this…wedge between them. One she wasn't sure she could fix with cookies and a positive attitude. "A spouse isn't usually someone you want to forget."

"It's not him I want to forget, really." She tried to put her smile back in place, feeling it fail. Her fingers bit into the underside of the vanity counter, needing something—anything—to keep her from slipping back into an empty headspace she didn't want to visit. "He died of cancer. While I was on my last tour. I tried to make it home—to be there for him, you know—but communications on assignment were spotty at best and arranging transport is hard when the enemy is shooting down anything they come across."

Tears broke through. The pain was cresting, sucking her under little by little, and she had nothing and no one to hold on to.

He took another step forward. "Jocelyn—"

"I know. Not exactly how you imagined your day would play out, right?" Years of practice had to be worth something. She swiped at her face, but getting rid of the physical evidence of her hurt wasn't enough. It'd never been enough. Turning to the mirror, she plastered that smile on her face. There. That was better. She could just make him out through the last layer of tears in her eyes. "First a bombing at your station, then a mercenary crying in front of you over her dead husband. Maybe next you'll get food poisoning from the dinner I put together. Wouldn't that be the icing on the cake?"

She had to get moving. Jocelyn grabbed for the first aid kit under the sink and started wrapping the blisters she'd broken open. Staying put gave the bad thoughts a chance to sneak in. They should've heard from Albuquerque's bomb squad by now. She had to finish those cookies for Elena and Cash, too. She should—

"Jocelyn, look at me." Baker's voice brought the downward cycle of to-do lists to a halt. He said her name as though it were the most beautiful word in his world, as though right then he saw who she really was. Not a mercenary. Not Carville. Just Jocelyn. Something behind her rib cage convinced her that he could fix everything with that single shift between them, but that wasn't how the world worked. How *grief* worked. No amount of pity was going to change the past.

But she still found herself locking her gaze on his.

Baker offered her his hand, palm up. Inviting. "I want to show you something."

He was giving her a choice to be touched, and appreciation nearly outpaced a rush of possibilities that crashed through her. She'd spent every day since getting the news that Miles hadn't survived his disease learning new languages, recipes, combat techniques and dozens of other experiences, but she couldn't imagine what a small-town police chief would want to show her.

She slipped her hand into his. His skin was bruised, cut, scabbing, harsher than she'd expected. But real. Baker dragged her free of the bathroom and toward the wall-to-ceiling window on the other side of her room. From here she could just make out Alpine Valley with the west end of the town peeking out from the canyon guarding it on both sides. An oasis in the middle of the New Mexican desert.

"You see that collection of buildings out there?" Radiant heat bled through the tinted panes of glass, but it was nothing compared to the warmth spreading through her hand. "Just outside of the canyon mouth?"

She focused everything she had on finding what he wanted her to see. Her heart pounded double-time in expectation of a full-blown breakdown as sadness worked through her, but the fear that usually rode on its coattails never came. As though their physical connection was holding her steady. "I see a barn, maybe a house. Though I'm not sure who lives there."

"I do." The window tint wasn't enough to block the sunset from highlighting all the small changes in his expression. "The barn, the house, the land. Three acres."

"So you're not as homeless as you led me to believe earlier?" She tried to make out the property lines to mentally gauge Baker's private kingdom, but there didn't seem to be anything but dirt and emptiness surrounding the structures. Dread pooled in her gut. "Why have you been crashing at the station for the past few months?"

"My sister and I had big plans to move out west and buy up land here in New Mexico. We were going to raise horses and start a bed and breakfast." He stared out at the land, not really here with her. "Took us a lot longer than it should have, but neither of us had built anything in our lives. We had to learn as we went. And buying up horses?" A scoff released the pressure of the moment. "Man, we were suckered into paying more than we should have, but we didn't care. We just wanted a place that was our own. Away from the chaos of the city. Somewhere we could hear ourselves think."

Why was he telling her this? "The two of you must be close."

"We were. Spent every second of our days together.

Well, almost. There were times we got on each other's nerves because we were overheated, sunburned and hungry from working the land all day, but we'd still sit down to dinner every night as though nothing had happened." His grip tightened around her hand. "The last time I saw her was during one of those stupid arguments. I don't even remember what I was so mad about. Guess it doesn't matter now, though."

Her mouth dried. "The last time you saw her?"

"About two weeks into getting the place off the ground, the cartel came calling. Talking some BS about how they owned the land we built on." Baker shifted his weight between both feet, his attention still out the window. She recognized the agitation for what it was: an attempt to distract himself. "Come to find out they'd set up one of their delivery routes straight through the property and weren't too keen on the idea someone had moved in on their territory. But we weren't just going to get up and leave."

"What happened?" In truth, she already knew the answer. Knew this story—like her own—didn't have a happy ending. How could it?

Baker locked that penetrating gaze on hers. "They burned everything we built to the ground. And took my sister right along with it."

HE HADN'T TOLD anyone about Linley before.

Not even his own deputies, but he didn't trust them anyway. Not after discovering one of his own had been working for the very people Baker despised. Of course, there'd been rumors. Questions as to why an outsider like him would want to suddenly apply for the position of chief of police. They hadn't trusted him. Still didn't. Not really. But he'd live up to his promise to protect the people of Alpine Valley. Especially from cartels like the one that had destroyed his life.

Baker memorized the rise and fall of the landscape as they shot across the desert inside Jocelyn's SUV. Surrounded by miles of desert, Alpine Valley had provided life to an entire nature preserve. Trees over a hundred feet tall crowded in around the borders and protected the natural hot springs and centuries-old pueblos tucked into the canyons. It was beautiful. Not in the same way he'd loved the leaves in the fall back east or watched snow pile up outside in his parents' backyard. There was honestly nothing but cracked earth, weeds and cacti as far as the eye could see.

But it was home now.

What had Linley called it? An oasis to forget their problems. If only that had been true.

"We need a plan." Baker turned his attention back to the file on his lap—the bombing outside of Ponderosa. Jocelyn had gone the extra mile to call in a favor from their department there, giving them full access to the case. They could dance around the present all they wanted with dark personal confessions and frank observations, but it wasn't going to change the fact that a bomb—most likely linked to the cartel—had been left in his station. Just as one had been left for the Ponderosa chief to find. "Albuquerque's bomb squad isn't going to like us just showing up on scene. There are protocols to follow so we don't disturb the evidence."

"It's all taken care of." Her hand—ringless, he couldn't help but notice—kept a light grip on the steering wheel as she maneuvered them along the familiar street lined with flat-roofed homes, rock landscaping and a few porch lights.

"What do you mean?" he asked.

Jocelyn didn't answer as she pulled into the parking lot that used to hold a much larger police station than what was left behind. Crime scene tape cut off access to approaching vehicles, but his cruiser was still parked outside the makeshift perimeter. She pulled the SUV beside it.

He'd reached out to his deputies to give them the rundown of what'd happened. It didn't matter that their station was sporting a sunroof nobody had wanted. Alpine Valley PD didn't get to take a vacation from answering calls. Though now his remaining two deputies would be answering and responding to calls for the foreseeable future from the town rec center. Good a place as any.

"Looks like the courts are barred from working out of their half of the building," he said.

"Standard procedure. Fire and Rescue doesn't want to run the risk of evidence contamination, even from people who know how important that evidence is in a case." Jocelyn put the vehicle into Park. "The fire marshal is waiting for us."

"You called Gary?" Baker shoved out of the SUV,

a little worse for wear. Hell, his whole body hurt from this morning's events. How did Jocelyn do it— moving as though she hadn't been impaled by a piece of debris as she pulled something from the back seat?

Gravel crunched under his boots as he followed the short path from the asphalt to the base of the station stairs. "I can't even get him to return my calls. Seems he doesn't agree with my choice in baseball teams. Though I'm not sure why he would take that so personally."

"You just have to know how to make him talk." She produced a plate of plastic-wrapped goods and grabbed her phone. With the swipe of her thumb, she raised the phone to her ear and rasped in a thick, Russian accent, "I have what you asked for."

She hung up. Waiting.

"Are we in the middle of delivering a ransom payment I don't know about?" Movement registered from the corner of the station to Baker's right. Instant alert had him reaching for his sidearm. Then recognition tendriled through him as Alpine Valley's fire marshal hauled his oversized frame closer. He relaxed a fraction. "Gary."

"Chief." Not Baker. Seemed grudges died hard with this one. Gary cut his gaze to Jocelyn, and the marshal's overall demeanor lost its bite. Yeah, she had the tendency to do that—ease into a person's subconscious and replace any darkness with rainbows and silver linings. "I believe you have something for me."

She handed off the plate as though embroiled in

an illegal trade. "Fresh batch of oatmeal. No raisins. They're all yours."

"You got ten minutes before Albuquerque wants me to check in." Gary had suddenly lost the ability to make eye contact, his entire focus honed in on the disposable plate in his hand.

"Thanks. We won't be long," Baker said.

The marshal didn't bother answering as he headed for his pickup across the street.

Baker motioned her ahead of him. "Seems you have your fingers in all the pies around here."

"Like I said, you just have to know how to get people to talk." Jocelyn took the lead up the stairs and produced a blade from one of her many cargo-pant pockets. The woman was better prepared than an Eagle Scout.

Cutting through the sticker warning trespassers of what waited for them if they were caught breaking into a crime scene, she braced her foot against one corner of the door to let him by. "With Gary, it's straight through his stomach. He kept coming back for my oatmeal cookies at the fundraiser last year. Later, I found a pile of discarded raisins in the parking lot."

"Here I thought the best way to a man's heart was through his third and fourth ribs." He unholstered his flashlight from his duty belt, then maneuvered past her, though he couldn't help but brush against her as he did. The physical contact eased the unsettled part of him that knew he was breaking a dozen different laws crossing into this crime scene, which he'd have to answer for, but the clock was ticking. The bomb squad's investigation could last days, maybe weeks. Possibly even months, if Chief Andrew Trevino's murder was anything to go by. They didn't have that kind of time—this was the first lead he'd had on Sangre por Sangre in months. He couldn't let it die.

Once inside, Baker punched the end of the flashlight, and a beam cut across the charred, debris-coated carpeting. "You always been able to read people like that?"

"I have a good sense for it." Jocelyn followed along the path through the building that the bomb squad had cleared for techs. She walked past what used to be the small kitchenette the former dispatcher had set up opposite the evidence room. "I see you more as a home-cooked-meal kind of guy."

"What gives you that impression?" The bitter scent of fire lodged in the back of his throat. Caustic. Suffocating. Baker felt his heart rate tick up a notch. He blinked to focus on the scene in front of him, but there were too many similarities. Sweat broke out across his forehead.

"You turned down my cranberry-lemon cookies this morning." Jocelyn's voice warbled there at the end. "And considering you've been crashing in a police station trailer armed with nothing but a microwave, I'd bet that dinner we had earlier hit the spot."

Baker couldn't move, couldn't speak. Every cell in his body put its energy into studying a half-destroyed coffee stirrer, and he lost any ability to get his lungs to work.

"Baker?" His name sounded distant. Out of reach.

Gravity held him hostage in that one spot despite the left side of his brain trying to catch up to the right. The flavor of smoke changed, contorting into something more acidic and nauseating. He took a step forward, though the layout of the station had vanished. He was walking toward the barn. What was left of it, at least. Intense heat still clung to the charred remains, flicking its tongue across his skin. "Linley?"

His shallow breathing triggered a wave of dizziness. She wasn't here. She couldn't be here. Because if the cartel had done this… No. He couldn't think like that. Baker took another step, his boots sinking deep into mud. The barn door nearly fell off its hinges as he wrenched it to one side. The entire building was about to crash down around him. All of this damage couldn't be from the result of a random fire. This was something far more explosive.

"Baker."

He knew that voice. Well enough to pull him up short. It whispered on the ash-tainted air around him. Like he could reach out and grab onto it. Jocelyn?

"Can you hear me?"

The fragment of memory jumped forward. To him standing in front of the body positioned in the center of the barn. Nothing about the remains resembled his sister, but he knew the cartel had done this. That they'd kept their word to burn his entire world to the ground if he didn't comply with their demands. And he'd let it happen. All because he'd gone into town for more hay.

Fury and shame and grief clawed through him as he sank to his knees. "I'll find them. Every single one of them. I give you my word… I'll make them pay."

"Baker!" Strong chocolate-brown eyes centered in his vision, replacing the horrors. Jocelyn fisted both hands into his uniform collar and crushed her mouth to his.

The past dissolved from right in front of him, replaced by physical connection tethered to reality. Her mouth was soft—hesitant—on his. The horrors clinging to the edges of his memory were displaced by the mint taste of her toothpaste and the slight aroma of oatmeal cookies. Baker lost himself in the feel of her mouth against his. On the slight catch of the split in her lip.

It was absolutely the most inappropriate thing to do in the middle of a crime scene, but his heart rate was coming back down. He had sensation back in his hands, and he latched on to Jocelyn as though he'd lose this grasp in the present if he didn't. The helplessness consuming him from the inside crawled back into the dark void he'd walled away. Until there was nothing left but her.

She settled back onto her heels, a direct mirror of his position on the floor. Her exhale brushed the underside of his jaw, and that simple rush to his senses was all it took. Jocelyn's eyes bounced between both of his, concern and fear and something like affection spiraling in the depths. "You with me?"

"Yeah." Baker tightened his hold on her vest. Because she was the only real thing he had. "I'm with you."

Chapter Five

Well, wasn't that just the milk to her cookies?

Jocelyn pried her grip from Baker's uniform collar and put a bit of distance between them. She'd kissed him, and in the moment, it'd been all she could think of to snap him out of whatever he'd been reliving. But now… Now there was a pressure in her chest reminding her that everything she touched died. House plants. Friendships. Her husband.

Shame burned through her as she tried to smooth the imprints of her hold from the fabric of his uniform. "I'm sorry. I…didn't know what else to do. You weren't answering, and I thought—"

"It's okay." Baker seemed to come back to himself then, but she couldn't help but wonder if his mind would pull him back into that terrifying void with the slightest reminder of what he'd been through.

She'd always known people who'd survived trauma—in war, in their own homes, as children or adults—could be caught in the suffocating spiral of PTSD, but the chief of police had never crossed her mind. And now his assumption that she suffered from post-traumatic stress made sense. It wasn't one of his deputies he'd been talking about who experienced nerve-wracking flashbacks. It was *him*. And she'd dragged him straight into a similar scene to what he'd witnessed.

"I shouldn't have brought you back here," she said.

He was still holding on to the shoulders of her vest. Gauging his surroundings, Baker finally let go. Yet he struggled to stay on his feet. Stable but weak. As though the past had taken everything he had left for itself. "I'm fine. It hasn't happened in a while. It just caught me off guard."

She reached out, resting her hand on his arm. She'd seen physical contact work in the field before. "If you need to wait in the car, I can go through—"

"I'm not leaving." There was a violence in his voice she hadn't heard until then. Just as she'd responded to him after he'd touched her mouth. It was reflected in his eyes as he seemed to memorize the scene around them. "I can do this."

Shame, guilt, helplessness—it all echoed through her just as it did him, and Jocelyn backed off. His response made sense. Fellow soldiers who'd lived through what could only be described as the worst days of their lives on tour kept going back, comforted by the very horrors that had scarred and disconnected them. Baker wouldn't admit defeat to the ambushing sights, sounds and smells in his head. No matter how unhealthy or unexpected. Because without them, he had nothing.

They were similar in that respect, and her heart

wanted to fix it. To make everything better. But she couldn't even help herself. How was she supposed to help him?

"Okay." Jocelyn swiped clammy hands down her pants. It'd been jarring and terrifying to see a man as confident and driven as Baker shut down right in front of her, but deep down she knew he wouldn't let it affect this investigation. The marshal had given them ten minutes inside the scene. She wasn't sure how much time they had left. They had to keep moving. "I'll see what I can find around the evidence closet."

She didn't wait for an answer. The hollow floor threatened to collapse from her added weight, but she kept to the path that the bomb squad had charted.

"Jocelyn, hold on." His hand encircled her arm, and she turned into him, though not out of some fight-or-flight instinct she didn't have control over. Because she wanted to. The flashlight beam cut across the floor from where he'd dropped it a few minutes ago, casting his expression in a white-washed glow. "I..."

Words seemed to fail him then. This man who fought for everyone in this town but himself. He didn't have to say the words. Despite the distance they'd kept lodged between themselves and the rest of the world, invisible connections were forged through survival. That was what they'd done today. Survived. And in that single act, she found herself more in line with Baker than she'd thought possible.

"I know. It's okay." She tried to put that smile

back in place. The one that could save the world, according to her husband. No matter what had been going on in their lives or how bad the pain had gotten from treatment, all he'd needed was that smile. And in the end, it was all he'd asked for, according to his nurses. But she hadn't been there.

The muscles around her mouth wavered. "We're all just trying to navigate the same road to healing," she said. "Every once in a while, we take a wrong turn or end up going in reverse. But that's why I'm glad you're here with me, in the passenger seat. Helping me navigate."

She slipped free of his hold, almost desperate to prove she could be his navigator in turn. That she could find something—anything—in this mess to give him some sense of peace. Squaring her shoulders, Jocelyn kept to the perimeter of where the blast had originated.

The bomb squad most assuredly had been through all of this. They would've spent hours trying to piece the device back together to identify its creator through a signature or fingerprint. But everything else would've had to wait. She took in the outline of the hole blasted through the far wall and low corner of what used to be a closet. The moments leading up to the blast played out as clearly as if they'd happened mere minutes ago, rather than hours.

Maverick had sniffed out the bomb's components in a box stacked at the back of a bottom shelf. It'd been a clever hiding place. But why there? "The evidence room."

"What did you say?" Baker kept his footsteps light as he carved a path through the makeshift kitchenette.

"Ponderosa's chief of police—Trevino—was killed with a bomb strapped to the underside of his pickup truck. There was no doubt that whoever set the device had targeted him. His wife had her own vehicle, and their kids were raised and grown. Moved out of state to start their own families." Her mouth couldn't keep up with her theory—as it did sometimes when her mind raced ahead in a recipe she'd memorized but her hands didn't work that fast. "The device from this morning was planted here. In the station. Where anyone could walk in."

He closed the distance between them, his arm making contact with the back of her vest. Just the slightest pressure, but enough to elicit a response. "You and Jones were convinced the bombing was meant for me. Now you're saying it wasn't?"

"Did you see the device this morning?" she asked.

Baker stilled, his gaze narrowing as she practically watched him replay the events of the day. There was still a hint of sweat at his temple. Evidence the tin man was all too human. "No. Maverick was in the way. He was sniffing around…an evidence box."

"It was on the bottom shelf. You remember?" She tried coming up with the case numbers marked on the outside, but there were still gaps in her memory from when her head had been lodged at the far wall. "Albuquerque's bomb squad is working off our assumption the device was meant for you. They'll put everything into putting what they can find of the bomb back together, but what if it was actually planted to destroy whatever was in that box? To stop a case from moving forward?" Her voice hitched with excitement. "Think about it. There are countless other places they could've set that bomb to get to you. Why would they purposely choose a box stashed on the bottom shelf of the evidence room unless they wanted to make sure no one could put the pieces back together?"

"Makes sense." Baker stared at the space where the floor should've been. "Question is, which case would they have wanted to destroy?"

"Did you have any active cases running on the cartel? Maybe one of their soldiers or an incident that occurred within Alpine Valley town borders?"

"Son of a bitch." Baker took a step back, scrubbing a hand down his face. "I should've seen it before now."

"You had a case," she said. "What was it?"

"Cartel lieutenant. Guy named Marc De Leon. We arrested him about three months ago. He'd taken to strapping a bomb to a woman's chest after torturing her for a couple hours. Best we could get from him, she was a random target. Unfortunately, she didn't survive, and the extent of her injuries kept us from identifying her. We've searched missing persons reports and interrogated the bastard any chance we could, but it's gotten us nowhere. Everyone just calls her Jane Doe." Sorrow dipped his voice into a whisper. "We could prove he was at the scene. Dead to rights. Found his fingerprints on the weapon he left behind. I picked him up on foot just outside of town covered in blood within a couple hours. It was easy to connect him back to the cartel through his priors. The lawyers are going at it right now, trying to claim some insanity defense, but it's not working. He knew exactly what he was doing when he killed her."

She'd heard about the raid. Known the town had nearly burned to the ground the night that another lieutenant had ordered his men to bring Elena Navarro and her eight-year-old brother, Daniel, to him. They'd torn apart families, destroyed homes and shops and set Alpine Valley right back under their control. By fear and intimidation. But now Baker was adding murder to the list. Why hadn't she known about this before tonight?

"The case wasn't going away. What better way to get your man off the hook than to send in your resident bomber to destroy all the evidence?" she said.

"Yeah, well. They got what they wanted, didn't they? We had the knife. We had his fingerprints, witness statements, GPS from his phone that put him in that house at the time of the raid." Baker kicked at a half-cremated box that hadn't gotten caught in the blast. "All destroyed. The prosecutor won't be able to do a damn thing about it, and that woman's family gets nothing. No sense of closure. No justice."

Her heart hurt at the idea of the victim's family knowing what'd happened to her but never being able to move on. Because Baker was there, too. Haunted by what'd happened to his sister, never finding peace.

Never being able to move on from the past. Jocelyn wanted that for him. A chance to heal, to live his own life apart from the horrible trauma that'd taken away everything he'd loved.

And there was only one way to do it.

She stepped to his side, staring down at the singed hole where the evidence room used to be. It wasn't just Marc De Leon's case that'd been destroyed but all of them. Dozens of victims who'd never see the resolution they deserved. "Lieutenants like De Leon are indispensable. It takes years of loyalty and trust to rise up the ranks. It's what he knows about the cartel's operation that they'd go out on a limb to save, but that doesn't make men like him untouchable."

"You sure about that?" he asked.

"Yeah." Jocelyn breathed in smoke-heavy air, mentally preparing for the war they were about to start. "I am."

HE WAS BACK at square one.

The promise of a new lead in his sister's murder was wearing thin. Pain radiated up his side as the SUV's shocks failed to navigate the uneven landscape. He'd once believed Alpine Valley was where he belonged, that his future rested here in miles of desert, star-streaked skies and protective canyons. Somewhere he could build a future.

He didn't have a future anymore.

Not until Sangre por Sangre paid for what they'd done. To him, to the residents of his town. To the hundreds of future victims they would discard in a power struggle to gain control. It wasn't just about what'd happened to Linley or that lieutenant trying to squeeze himself out of a murder charge. It was *all* of it. The constant threat and the repercussions of a cartel's choices determined who would live at the end of the day and who wouldn't. And Baker couldn't accept that. These people deserved better, and he wasn't going to stop. Not until every last man and woman connected to the cartel was behind bars or six feet under.

The rush of adrenaline he'd suffered at the smallest inkling of a threat refused to let go. It was tensing his hands until he found it nearly impossible to release. His body had yet to get the signals there wasn't any actual danger right in front of him, and there was only one way to force it back into submission.

"I need you to do me a favor." His voice failed on the last word. Exhaustion had gotten the best of him long before now, but he was somehow still holding it together. They were coming up on the road that would either take them back to Socorro or to the edge of town. "Turn right up here at the T."

Jocelyn's mouth parted in the dim light given off by the SUV's controls behind the steering wheel. The slightest change in facial expression spoke volumes. She knew exactly what he was asking, and she was the only one who could help. "Are you sure?"

"I just need…" He didn't know what he needed. Something familiar? Baker didn't have the capacity to explain right then. The gnawing hollowness in his chest wouldn't let him. "I'm sure."

She navigated north.

He'd driven this way so many times, he could practically feel his breath coming easier as he anticipated every bump in the dirt road. But it wasn't enough. A war between getting relief and putting himself at risk raged as the rough outline of the structures separated from the surrounding darkness up ahead.

"You can stop here," he said.

Momentum kept his upper body moving forward as Jocelyn brought the SUV to a full stop outside the cattle gate, but the pain stayed at a low simmer. "I'll just be a few minutes."

"You don't have to go in there alone." Her hand shot out as he shouldered the passenger side door open, clamping on to the top of his thigh. The contact should've set him on high alert, but there was something about Jocelyn Carville that put him at ease. "I could come with you."

His automatic answer rushed to the front of his mind. He should shut her down, take the time he needed to get his head back in the game. But the logical part of him understood she'd already seen him at his worst, that walking into that house without support could break him.

Baker let his hand slip from the door. "Yeah. Okay."

The vehicle's headlights guided them to the gate. A chill ran through the air. A storm was on its way in, the first few drops collecting along the top of the gate. Baker grabbed for the padlock securing the gate to the frame and took out his key, twisting it in the lock. The chain hit the dirt, and he swung the gate open. "Welcome to my humble abode."

Gravel crunched under their feet as they hiked the empty driveway. The barn sat in the distance, more than half of the structure gone from the explosion. Its rugged outline stood stark against the backdrop of the last bit of blue behind the mountains. But the house was still intact. The single story was exactly as he'd left it. Tan stucco practically glowed in the beaming moonlight and highlighted the black window casings, two-car garage and front door. Mid-century metal floral details held up one corner of the porch, matching the color of the exterior of the house. It was a weird, old addition on a brand-new build, but Linley had insisted. Now he couldn't imagine taking it out.

Baker hauled himself up the front steps and gripped the front door handle with one hand. The oversized picture window stared back at him from his left, and he couldn't help but let his senses try to penetrate through the glass. As though his sister would be waiting for him to come home on the other side as she had so many times before.

Jocelyn followed his hesitant footsteps. "We can still turn back…"

No. As much as he wanted to pretend the past didn't affect the present, his body kept score.

Baker slid the key into the deadbolt. "Don't you know by now, Carville? There is no going back. Not for people like us."

Hinges protested as he pushed inside. A wall

of stale air drove down his throat. The breeze cut through the opening in the front door and ruffled the plastic coating the furniture, and an instant hit of warmth flooded through him. He tugged the key from the deadbolt and moved aside to let Jocelyn over the threshold, flipping on the entryway light.

"It's much bigger than it looks from the outside." She carved a path ahead of him. Her bootsteps echoed off the hardwood floors and tall ceilings. Taking in the stretch of the great room and the fireplace mantel he and his sister had crafted by hand, Jocelyn moved as though she'd been here before. "You built all this?"

Baker shut out the cold, letting the entire space seep into his bones. "Me and my sister. I did most of the heavy lifting. She picked out all the extras. The color of the floors, paint on the walls. A time or two I'd needed her help framing out the closet or installing the toilets. She really could do it all."

"What was her name?" Jocelyn carefully ran her hand the length of the mantel, as though she knew that was the final piece he'd installed in this house.

"Linley." It'd been so long since he'd let himself speak her name, it tasted foreign on his tongue. Though not as bitter as he'd expected. "She had a talent for stuff like this. I always told her she could be a designer, but she loved horses more."

Jocelyn intercepted the single framed photo and lifted it off the mantel. One taken of him and Linley, each holding hammers in a ridiculous power pose in front of their finished project. "Is this her?"

"Yeah." He maneuvered around the sectional, his thigh brushing over plastic, and took the frame from her. "This was the day we officially finished the house. We were trying to pose like those brothers on the renovation show, but we couldn't stop laughing because every time we set my phone up to take the picture on top of this bag of concrete, it fell off. I ended up cracking my screen, but we somehow managed to make it work."

Heat seared through him as Jocelyn's arm settled against his side. The need for something familiar didn't seem to have as great a hold on him. Not with her here. "She looks like you. Same eyes. Same smile. She's stunning."

"Does that mean you think I'm stunning, then, too?" Where the hell had that come from? And what did he care what she thought of him?

"I wouldn't call you ugly." Jocelyn backed off, hands on her hips, and he swore a flush rushed up her neck. "Unless you piss me off."

Baker pressed his thumb into the corner of the framed photo. "Well, I wouldn't want that. Who else is going to feed me something other than prepackaged ramen noodles?"

Her smile did more to light up the room than the light-fan combination above them. "Oh, is that all I'm good for? You got what you wanted out of me, and now I'm back to being the mercenary who bakes?"

"Nah. Once you survive a bombing together, you can never go back to being acquaintances." Baker set the photo back on the mantel. He liked this. The back and forth they'd shared since this morning. It came with a weird sensation of…lightness. Like he'd been cutting himself off from everything that made him happy as some kind of penance. "You heard from Animal Control?"

"Yeah. Socorro's vet picked Maverick up a little while ago," she said. "He's got a slight limp, but for the most part he's fine. Should be back to normal in a couple days. Just needs a bit of rest."

"He's not the only one." He prodded at the lump behind his left ear. It'd kept itself in check for most of the day, but after coming here, his nerves had reached their end. "If the hospital hadn't told me otherwise, I would've sworn I cracked my head open."

"Your head hurts?" She moved in close. Close enough he caught a hint of color in her eyes before she raised her hands to him. Angling the side of his head toward her, she framed his jaw with one hand while sliding her fingertips against his scalp. "I don't see any changes in the bruise patterns since we left the hospital. We've been running on fumes most of the day. I'm sure your body is just trying to get you to slow down. I can keep watch if you want to grab a couple hours of sleep."

His scalp tightened at the physical contact. At the way she kept her touch light. It shouldn't have meant anything, but for a man starved of the smallest comforts and pleasures since he'd lost everything, it hit harder than he'd expected. And he liked it—her touching him. "You noticed my bruise patterns?"

"Isn't that what partners are for?" Jocelyn moved to

retreat, only he wasn't ready for the withdrawal. "To notice each other's wounds and then poke and prod at them?"

Baker caught her wrist, tracing the edge of gauze across the back of her hand. Warning speared through him. Because just as he'd found himself reliving the worst seconds of his life back at the station, Jocelyn had her own regrets. Of not being there for her husband when he'd died. One touch was all it'd taken to send her running, and he didn't want that. For the first time in ages, he couldn't stand the thought of being alone. "I'm pretty sure if I prod your wound, you're going to bleed out."

Her breath hitched. "That's possibly the most romantic thing anyone has ever said to me."

A laugh took him by surprise, and he released her. A frenzy of feeling rushed into his hands, as though his body had been craving the feel of her skin.

"I'm glad you brought me here." She threaded an escaped strand of hair back behind her ear. Such a soft thing to do in light of all the weapons and armor she wore. A welcome contradiction to everything he thought he'd known about her. "I can tell how much you love this home."

"Home." The word tunneled through the drift-like haze clouding his overtired brain, but he forced himself to focus on the present. "Back at the station you said it takes years for lieutenants like Marc De Leon to rise up Sangre por Sangre's ranks, that the organization tends to protect them because of what they know. The cartel provides their lieutenants security, income, even compounds. But that they aren't untouchable."

"Yeah," she said. "There have been times when the lieutenants let the power and ego go to their heads. They take on their own agenda and use cartel resources as their own personal arsenal. I've seen it before. The soldiers—no matter how far they are up the ladder— are usually punished by upper management."

"You mean executed." He latched on to her arms as the burn of anticipation sparked beneath his skin. "If our theory about who planted that bomb at the station is right, that means the cartel ordered Benito Ramon to destroy evidence De Leon killed that woman. They know he stepped out of line, but they haven't put him down. Why?"

Jocelyn shifted her weight, the first real sign that the day was getting to her as much as it had to him. "I don't know. It makes sense they'd want to tie up that loose end before it unraveled their operation. Unless…he actually was ordered to kill her."

"We need De Leon to give us the name of the bomber." Releasing his hold on her, he tried to put everything he understood about the cartel into play. "And I think I just figured out a way to get Sangre por Sangre to stop protecting him."

Chapter Six

Life was starting to feel like a box of cookies.

Some she couldn't wait to bite into. Peanut butter. A really soft chocolate chip. Maybe a homemade Oreo. Others she'd always leave in the bottom of the tin. Peppermint. Orange. Even worse, orange peppermint. And this plan had an aftertaste that left a horrible bitterness in her mouth.

Jocelyn shoved the SUV into Park about a quarter mile from the house and cut the lights. It wasn't difficult to uncover Marc De Leon's home address, especially for Alpine Valley's chief of police. But being here—without backup—in the middle of the night pooled tightness at the base of her spine. She'd gone up against the cartel before. Using one of their lieutenants to flip on a bomber they believed to be the Ghost wasn't going to end the way Baker hoped.

"I don't see any movement or lights on in the compound," she said.

"Doesn't mean he's not there." A battle-ready tension she'd noted during the flashback that'd ambushed him at the station bled through his hands.

This was a bad idea. "Baker, I know you think you have to do this to find whoever blew up your station, but Socorro has ways of getting that information without—"

"Without what? Getting their hands dirty?" The muscles in his jaw ticked in the glow of the vehicle's control panel. "Not sure you know this, but most police work isn't done from a distance with unlimited resources and military equipment. Most of my job is climbing into the sandbox and uncovering the next lead myself. Marc De Leon is our best chance of confirming Benito Ramon is the Ghost, and I'm not leaving until he does."

Baker didn't wait for her response and ducked out of the SUV.

Damn it. He was going to charge in there with or without her. Maybe even get himself shot. Or worse. Jocelyn followed his silhouette to the front of the hood, then moved out of the vehicle. Taking on the cartel—no matter the angle—had only ever ended in blood. She wasn't going to let him walk in there unprepared. "Then you're going to need some of those resources."

Rounding to the cargo area, she punched the button to release the door. She flipped the heavy black tarp back to expose the full range of artillery at her disposal.

"You've been driving around with this back here the whole time?" His low whistle preceded Baker's hand reaching for the nearest weapon—an M4 automatic rifle. "I could have you arrested for some of these. You know how to use all this?"

Nothing like witnessing shock and awe when confronted with the fact the woman driving you around could do more than bake cookies. "It's all legal. Socorro operatives are licensed and trained with a variety of weapons. There isn't anything in this trunk I don't know how to handle." She gestured to the M4. "You'll want to be careful with that one. The trigger is sensitive. Extra magazines are closer to the back seat."

He collected what he could carry. "Why do I get the sense you've been holding out on me?"

"Funny coming from a man who's referred to me as a mercenary on more than one occasion." She armed herself with an extra magazine for the pistol holstered on her hip. More wasn't always better. Despite all of the resources and gear available, Jocelyn trusted herself over a gun in any situation. Because that was all she could count on at the end of the day.

"Yeah, well, I might have changed my mind over the past few hours." Baker threaded one arm through the gun's strap and centered the weapon over his sternum, barrel down like the good officer he was supposed to be.

She hauled the tailgate closed and locked the vehicle. Couldn't take the chances of someone else getting their hands on her gear. "You mean after I kissed you?"

"That helped." He seemed to be trying to steady himself with a few deep breaths. "You ready?"

"You really believe the only way to get to the Ghost is through De Leon?" Because the moment they crossed that property line, Sangre por Sangre would consider their visit an act of war. He had to know that.

He nodded. "Yeah. I do."

Her gut trusted his answer. It'd have to be good enough for her. She handed off a backup vest. "Then I'm ready."

They moved as one, keeping low and moving fast along the worn asphalt road. According to satellite imaging, the cartel lieutenant's property sat on the edge of a cliff looking down into Alpine Valley, though she could only see the front of the compound from here. Thin, modern cuts of rock, pristinely stacked on top of each other, created a seven-foot barrier between them and the main house. Hopping over the fence at one of the distant corners was the smartest strategy, but Jocelyn couldn't dislodge the warning in her gut. Like they'd be walking right into an ambush.

They each pulled back at the gate and scanned the interior of the compound. Heart in her throat, she stilled. No floodlights. Or any movement from a guard rotation. No signs of life as far as she could tell. Not inside the house, either. This didn't make sense. The cartel wouldn't leave their lieutenant unprotected. "There's no one here."

She set her palms against the gate and shoved. Metal hinges protested as the heavy structure swung inward. Something wasn't right. No security-conscious cartel operative would leave the gate unlocked. Jocelyn caught sight of a security camera mounted above her left shoulder, but the LED light wasn't working. Was the power out?

Baker paused before crossing over the threshold. "Guess that makes our job easy, then."

She didn't trust *easy*, but they didn't have a whole lot of choice here, either. She crossed beyond the gate. Every cell in her body ratcheted into high alert. Waiting for…something.

Thick fruit trees branched out from their line along the driveway and clawed at her exposed skin and hair as she headed for the front door. Pavers and old-world exposed beams created a feeling found nowhere else other than New Mexico. Drying chilis hung from beside columns built of the same stone as the wall they'd bypassed. Black sconces—unlit—stood as sentinels on either side of a wood double door. Marc De Leon was out on bail, but this place was a ghost town as far as she could tell.

"I don't like this," she said.

"I'm starting to understand what you mean." Baker nudged the toe of his shoe against the front door. It swung inward without much effort. "Ladies first?"

Once they stepped into the house, there was no going back. No reason she could give to Ivy and the rest of the team for explaining why she'd breached a cartel lieutenant's home without authorization.

Jocelyn centered the man at her side in her line of vision, but the shadows were too thick here. All she could see was that look on his face as he'd stood helpless in the middle of the station, caught up in the horrors his mind craved to process. It spoke of how little he'd let himself feel since losing his sister. His life had stopped moving forward that day the cartel had come calling. She could see it in the way he pushed everyone away, including her, in the way he committed himself to finding any angle, any strategy to catch Sangre por Sangre in the smallest infraction.

"You believe the Ghost is responsible for Linley's death." She wasn't sure where the thought had come from, but it explained a lot. Why he wanted to keep their little operation off the books, why he was so determined to get to De Leon.

Baker didn't answer, and he didn't need to. She already knew.

"Stay behind me." She unholstered her weapon and took that step over the threshold. For Baker. There was no end to the war raging in her head, but she could help him win the one in his. "Whatever happens, I want you to get yourself out alive. Socorro will help."

He didn't bother arguing. Of the two of them, she was by far the most trained, and they both knew it. Jocelyn tried to force her senses to catch up to the darkness, but all she could make out was a window detail cut into the entryway wall ahead of her. They were dead center in a long hallway, cut off from seeing the spaces straight ahead. This would be the perfect angle for an ambush—unprotected on either side. But nobody jumped out from the shadows.

Moonlight punctured through the windows to

her left, and she found herself stepping across dark-
colored tiles in that direction for a better layout of
the house. The entryway hall ended abruptly, revealing an oversized living room on the other side. This
place was massive. Well over twenty thousand square
feet. There was no way they'd be able to search it
quickly. She memorized the configuration of individual sitting chairs and sofas. Untouched. Everything in its place.

"Where is everyone?" Jocelyn slowed her path
through the living room to the kitchen visible through
another window cut out at the end of the room. Her
heart threatened to beat straight out of her chest as
her reflection cast back at her from the large mirror
angled over a stone fireplace spanning the entire wall.

A significant part of her work in the military and
Socorro was based off being able to predict and antic-
ipate the needs of those around her, and she'd jumped
at the opportunity to take on Baker's personal demons instead of facing off with her own. But something wasn't right here. "We need to get out of here."

"Not yet." He made a move for the second entry
into the living room, weapon raised. "He's here. He
has to be here."

Baker was going off script. They were supposed
to stick together. They didn't know what waited inside the house. They could be walking into a trap.
Her brain grabbed for frantic imagines of her husband as Baker disappeared down the hall. Of Miles's
head supported by that silky white pillow in the cas-
ket. Of the wrinkle she couldn't get out of his suit no

matter how many times she'd tried. Of Baker's face replacing that of her husband's.

Jocelyn tried to suck in enough air to wash them out. It worked, but the pressure in her chest refused to let up. Holding her back. "Baker, wait."

The sound of shuffling cut through the darkness somewhere out of reach of her current position. She squeezed her sidearm between both hands. At the ready. Clearing the dining room, she moved into the kitchen. Another sitting room was attached to this space with a second set of furniture and a fireplace. She scanned every inch, but Baker wasn't here. "Damn it."

A breeze tickled the hairs on the back of her neck. She turned to face an open patio door.

And the silhouette waiting in the dark.

"Oh, good. You found the place."

A gunshot exploded.

Just before the pain took hold.

THERE WEREN'T ANY gunshots in his nightmares.

A groan worked through his chest. Baker eased onto his side. Cold floor bit into his skull and shoulders. Hell, his head hurt. A waft of smoke dove into his lungs and threatened to send him right back where he didn't want to be. Standing in the middle of his barn, taking in the aftermath of what the cartel had done.

He pressed one palm into the floor—no, this didn't feel like ceramic—trying to get his bearings. He rolled onto his back. And met nothing but a starry sky. Dirt infiltrated his clothing and worked under his fingernails. He was outside. The smoke was coming from his uniform. He blinked to try to get his brain rewired. The last thing he remembered was being inside the compound. How the hell…

"Jocelyn?"

"Is that her name?" an unfamiliar voice asked. "Sorry to say I didn't ask before I pulled the trigger."

Baker's instincts had him reaching for the weapon strapped against his chest. Only it wasn't there. He went for his service weapon. Empty. He rolled onto one shoulder, unable to get his hands under him. He'd been bound. Zip ties. The vest he'd borrowed from Jocelyn was suddenly much heavier than he'd estimated. His belt was gone, too.

Using his weight to his advantage, he got to his feet. Agony ripped through his head, and he doubled over before stumbling a couple feet and hitting what felt like a cactus with one hand. The sting spread faster than he was expecting.

"You're going to want to take it easy. Can't imagine two concussions in twenty-four hours will be a walk in the park." Movement registered from his right. Or was it his left? Hard to tell with his brain in a blender. An outline solidified as a vehicle's headlights cut through the night. "I'd apologize for the theatrics, but your showing up here left me with little choice."

Baker shielded his eyes against the onslaught, dead center in the headlight's path. His head pounded in rhythm to his heartbeat. The logical part of his brain attempted to catalogue distinguishable features of the man in front of him, but the added light only made it more difficult. "Who the hell are you?"

"That's not what you really want to ask me, Chief." The outline set himself against the front of the hood of what looked like a pickup truck. Similar to Baker's.

The headache was easing. Not entirely, but enough to recall he'd been ambushed the second he'd stepped into the hallway of Marc De Leon's compound. His fingers curled into the center of his palms to counter the heat flaring up his spine, but he couldn't keep the growl out of his voice. "Where is Jocelyn?"

"Inside." A slight shift of weight was all Baker managed to take in with the amount of space between them. "I'm not sure if she's still alive, but in all honesty, I needed her out of the way. To get to you."

Still alive? Panic and a heavy dose of rage combined into a vicious cocktail that had Baker closing the distance between them. "You better pray she's alive."

Something vibrated against his chest.

He froze, grabbing for whatever was lodged against his rib cage.

"That's close enough, Chief." The figure ahead took his own step forward. An LED light lit up the man's hand, and another vibration went through Baker. "You know what this is?"

Son of a bitch.

"I'm going to guess it's not a box of chocolates." Baker was forced to back off. He was still wearing the vest Jocelyn had lent him, but it'd been altered. Turned into a weapon rather than a protection, and he was instantly reminded of the woman Marc De Leon had tortured and killed. With a vest just like this. Packed with explosives. A touch of a button—that was all it would take for the bomber to finish what he'd started.

"Let me guess," he said. "You set the bomb in my station."

The man raised his hands in surrender, all the while pinching that little detonator between his thumb and palm. "To be fair, I didn't expect you to make it out of there. Otherwise I wouldn't have had to go to all these lengths."

"You're the Ghost. Sangre por Sangre's go-to bomber. Sixteen—well, now seventeen—incidents over the span of two years. All this time, we've been thinking a man named Benito Ramon was responsible, but that was just another alias, wasn't it? Marc De Leon." The bomber he'd been looking for. Who'd set the device that'd brought down his future and killed his sister. Undeniable grief and rage flashed through every fiber of his being. He dared another step forward. The vibrating intensified in warning. "You took everything from me."

"I never liked that name. The Ghost. Always gave too much credit where none had been earned." De Leon straightened, matching Baker in height. The lack of accent was telling. Baker had always found it out of place during their interrogations. Not born and bred from within Sangre por Sangre, but an outsider. A hired gun. A true mercenary who killed on orders and walked away with his pockets all the heavier. "But since we're getting to know each other, here's what's going to happen. You're going to get in the truck, and when I push this button, you're going to be blown to pieces and lefts for Albuquerque's bomb squad to put back together, and we can all live happily ever after."

Not a chance. "If this was your pitch to Ponderosa's chief of police, I gotta tell you, it needs some work."

"Let me ask you something, Chief." De Leon inched closer, within reach, though the headlights made it impossible to decipher the bomber's features out here in the pitch black. "When you found your sister's body, what was the first thing you did? Scream? Cry? Or did you just stand there staring at her, trying to find some semblance of the woman she'd been beneath all that burnt skin?"

A tightness in his throat threatened to wrench away his control. Baker pressed his wrists against the zip ties until the edges cut into his skin. "Shut your damn mouth."

"You think you're the only one who's lost someone to Sangre por Sangre?" De Leon lost a bit of aggression in his voice. "My friend, you don't know what pain is. They might've taken your sister, but you didn't have to watch her suffer. You didn't have to hear her screams while they held you down and made you watch as she begged for you to help her. You got off lucky."

"Lucky. Right. You know what? I do feel lucky." The fire that'd been driving him since finding Linley bound with a flaming tire around her neck threatened to extinguish itself. No. The man in front of him was not an ally, and Baker sure as hell didn't trust a single word out of his mouth. "You've obviously been keeping tabs on me. Knew I'd be here, looking for the man who could give up the Ghost. You might have even connected the dots. My sister was killed by the cartel with a device just like the one the bomb squad recovered. Stood to reason this incident might be connected to hers. Hell, you even called me by my first name. Like we're friends."

De Leon didn't answer, as though sensing the rising flood churning inside of Baker.

Baker took a step forward, ignoring the vibration from the device pressed against his midsection. "You probably think you know me pretty well. My habits, my motives. Who I've talked to, how I spend my free time. But do you know why I took the job as Alpine Valley's chief of police?"

"Wasn't hard to fill in the blanks," De Leon said. "Anyone with half a brain can see you'd want to use your authority to get to the cartel."

"See, now that's where you're wrong." Baker strained against the zip ties. "I took the job because I was afraid of what I'd do to the man who killed my sister and burned down my barn with her horses inside when I found him."

He took another step forward. "So you're right. I am lucky. I didn't have to wait my entire life hunting for you." Baker pressed his knuckles together and snapped the zip ties in one clean break. "You were stupid enough to come after me yourself."

De Leon's laugh penetrated through the low ringing in Baker's ears. "That's quite the speech, Chief. I like the theater with snapping the zip ties, too, but you're forgetting one thing." He raised the detonator between them.

"You think that little black box scares me?" Adrenaline dumped into Baker's veins. Out here in cartel territory there were no rules, but time didn't bow down to anyone. Jocelyn was injured, possibly bleeding out, and the longer he faced off with the ghosts of his past, the higher the chance she didn't make it out of this alive. He grabbed on to the bastard's collar and dragged him close. "As long as you and I are together, you won't pull that trigger. You'll just end up killing yourself in the process."

Baker cocked his arm back and rocketed his fist forward.

De Leon dodged the attempt, then again as he threw a left. "You don't want to do this, Chief. It's not going to end the way you think."

The momentum thrust Baker into the hood of the truck.

"You know what? I think I really do." He spun back, ready for an attack, but it never came. Frustration and an overwhelming sense of desperation to make this right burned through him faster than the flames had singed his skin at the station. Shoving off the truck, he aimed his shoulder into De Leon's midsection and hauled the son of a bitch off his feet.

They hit the dirt as one.

And an explosion lit up the desert.

The compound was engulfed in a dome of bright flames, black smoke and hurling debris less than a quarter mile away.

"No." De Leon pried himself out from Baker's grip and shot to his feet. "I was talking about your partner."

A fist slammed into Baker's face. Once. Twice.

Lightning struck behind his eyes as a burst of heat expanded out from the blast site, paralyzing him at the realization that someone he cared about had been lost to the cartel all over again.

Chapter Seven

Raisin cookies that looked like chocolate chips was one of the main reasons she had trust issues.

Jocelyn hurled herself through the open patio door.

Barely conscious, she let herself get sucked beneath the surface of the outdoor pool as a wave of flames splintered out from the house.

The explosion punctured deep under the water and pressurized the air in her lungs and ears. Bubbles raced upward from all the nooks and crannies of her gear and tickled her skin along the way. Chlorinated water drove up her nose and into the back of her throat, but she wouldn't inhale. No matter how much her body wanted to.

A submersive shift reverberated through her as debris rained down from above. Covering her head as best she could, Jocelyn tried to wait it out, but she hadn't caught a full breath before going in.

Something heavy hit the water.

She forced her head up just before a section of the compound's protective wall sank directly over her.

She kicked as hard as she could against the pool's bottom to get out of the way, but her gear held her down. The wall landed on her right ankle. Her muted scream echoed in her own ears as the wall's weight crushed down on the bones between her foot and calf.

Wrapping both hands around her thigh, she pulled as hard as the bullet wound in her shoulder allowed. Flames lit up the surface of the water and highlighted strings of blood floating out of the wound. She'd been hit. Now she was pinned beneath the pool's surface and running out of air. An entire pool of water battled for domination as she pulled at her leg again. The pain spiraled down into her toes and suctioned a larger percentage of air.

The harder she fought, the sooner she'd drown. Debris settled in the bottom of the pool, and she grabbed for something—anything—she could use to wedge beneath the stone wall. Dirt and rock dodged her attempts to placate her survival instincts. Fire flickered above her as the remnants of the house settled.

Her heart thudded too hard at the base of her neck. Each pulse beat stronger than the one before it until she was sure her chest might explode from the effort. Jocelyn pressed her hands to her vest, searching her own gear. The pain in her chest was spreading. Panic sucked up oxygen in the process. Black tendrils encroached on her vision as her fingers hit something heavy in her belt. Her baton. It was all she could think of.

Frantic to make the agony stop, she ripped the tactical baton free. With too much force. The steel slipped from her grip and disappeared into the inky darkness beneath her. Pinching her eyes closed, she tried to feel for it but met nothing but the coarse coating used to protect pools from cracking. It scraped against her knuckles and lit up her dying nerves.

Her toes had lost feeling. The sensation was spreading up into her ankle and taking hold, but she couldn't let herself pass out. The moment she gave up, her body's automatic functions would kick her lungs to inhale. She'd drown within seconds. No. She had to find that baton.

Seconds slipped through her fingers as she stretched her wounded arm. Her fingertips hit something cylindrical and heavy in the initial pass, but it slipped out of reach. The bullet had torn straight through her shoulder. If she could just extend a bit more—

Unimaginable pain ricocheted through her arm and into her neck. She lost the last reserves of air in a silent scream, sinking deeper. She tried to leverage her free foot beneath her, but the angle was all wrong. She had no strength here. Groping for the baton a second time, she couldn't ignore the crushing weight pressing against her chest.

She was out of time. Out of options.

Jocelyn fought against the drugging pull of heaviness and kicked at the section of wall on her foot. It wouldn't budge. This couldn't be it. This couldn't be how she was going to die. Because she hadn't really given herself a chance to live.

The days, weeks and months after Miles's death had been spent in pure survival. She'd shut down the part of herself that could connect with others on a cellular level while outwardly portraying a woman who was trying to pull her team together. Truth was she'd gone numb inside a long time ago. But the past twenty-four hours had given her a purpose. Something—no, someone—to focus on. A puzzle to solve. One she wasn't ready to give up on yet.

Jocelyn leveraged her free foot into the bottom of the pool and shoved off with everything she had left. It would have to be enough. The last few air bubbles shook free of her clothing and escaped to the surface as she forced her arm against the torn muscles.

Her fingers brushed over the top of the baton.

She wrapped her grip around the solid metal and extended it to its full length. There was a chance the steel would crumple under the weight of the wall, but she had to try. She wedged the tip alongside her trapped ankle and, using both hands, forced her upper body to do something impossible.

The wall shifted upward.

Feeling rushed back into her foot, and Jocelyn dragged her leg free. Relief didn't have a hold on her as the weight of her vest and weapons countered her one-handed strokes. Her insides were eating at themselves, the lack of oxygen shutting down organ after organ in an attempt to save energy for her heart, brain and lungs.

The very same armor she'd donned to protect herself would be what killed her in the end. Jocelyn tore at the shoulder of her Kevlar vest and loosened its hold. Its familiar weight was lost to the darkness creeping along the bottom of the pool. She couldn't think, couldn't remember what she had to do next. Her boots felt too tight. They had to go. She let go of the baton and pulled her backup magazines and weapons from her pockets.

In a last attempt at survival, she kicked at the bottom of the pool. The momentum carried her upward with the help of one hand grabbing onto what felt like a thin ladder.

She broke through the surface. And gasped.

Her chest ached under the influx in oxygen. Jocelyn clung to the side of the pool. Exposed skin was instantly assaulted by heat from all sides, but she couldn't convince her body to move. Someone had shot her and left her for dead. It was only when she'd regained consciousness on the floor of the kitchen that she'd noted the thin wires strung throughout the exposed rafters of the house. The ones connected to a similar device Albuquerque's bomb squad was currently trying to piece back together.

Only much larger and a whole lot more complicated.

If she hadn't woken when she had…

Jocelyn clawed her upper body over the edge of the pool and collapsed—face down—onto debris-ridden cement. Chunks of stone and what used to make up Marc De Leon's compound bit into her face. Hell, she hurt, but she couldn't stop now. "Baker."

He'd been in the house with her. But had he made it out alive?

Dragging one knee beneath her, she pressed herself up. The compound was burning right in front of her eyes. Embers raced toward the sky with thick clouds of smoke.

A rumble vibrated underneath her, and thin cracks split the cement beneath her hands. "Oh, no." The compound sat on the edge of a cliffside looking over Alpine Valley. If the explosion had been strong enough...

Jocelyn shoved to her feet. Her balance failed, and she stumbled into a low wall that'd somehow managed to survive the blast.

This whole area was on the verge of collapse.

They had to get out of here.

"Baker!" She forced one busted foot in front of the other. Making out the remnants of what was left of the kitchen, she maneuvered around a turned-over hood vent and crossed into a house on its last legs. An exposed beam crashed off to her left and decimated the fireplace from the sitting room off the kitchen. Old tile flooring threatened to trip her up as she tried to re-create the layout of the house in her head. She'd lost Baker somewhere between the main living space and the bedrooms on the other side of the house.

"Baker...can you hear me?"

No answer.

Her heart stuttered at the thought of finding him in

this mess. The house groaned under its attempt to stay standing, but another rumble threw her into a half-failing wall between the kitchen and dining room.

"Baker, we have to get out of here!"

Smoke chased down her throat and silenced her voice. No amount of coughing dislodged the strangling feeling of nearly drowning in a cartel lieutenant's pool. Glass and rock cut into the bottoms of her bare feet as she launched herself down what used to be the hallway.

He had to be here.

"Where are you?" Covering her mouth and nose with her soaked T-shirt, she stumbled through the house's remains, but there was no sign of him.

Except… She pulled up short of the hallway leading to the bedrooms. He must've turned left out of the living room when she'd gone right. Because there, in the middle of a section of broken tile, flames were in the process of melting something shiny and gold. Something familiar.

Her breath left her all at once, as though she were back beneath the surface of the pool. Trapped. Deprived. In agony. She grabbed for a piece of charred wood and knocked the police badge out of the flames. But no amount of staring at it changed the dread pooled in her gut. Jocelyn searched the surrounding hallway as another groan escaped from the home's bones. "No. No, no, no."

There was no point in denying it.

The chief had been inside the compound when the bomb detonated.

A POINT WAS coming where his head wouldn't be able to take much more.

Baker pulled his chin away from his chest. Pain arced down his spine as he dragged his head back. His skull hit something soft. Cushioning. Prying his eyes open, he stared out over his truck's dashboard. A hint of gasoline added to the burn of smoke in his lungs from earlier. Must've spilled some the last time he'd gassed up.

Pins and needles pricked at his fingers and forearms, and he moved to adjust. But couldn't. Two sets of cuffs slid along the curve of the steering wheel. "What the hell?"

It took a few seconds to kick his senses into gear. This was his truck, but he hadn't driven out to the middle of the desert... Jocelyn had.

Fractures of fire, an explosion and the hole in his chest tearing wider jerked him into action. Baker wrenched against the cuffs, digging the metal into the skin along his wrists. He always carried a set of handcuff keys on him. He went for his slacks, but the chains linking the cuffs refused to give. Just short of reaching his pocket. Pressing his heels into the floor, he tried to lift his hips to his hands, but it was no use. The seat had been moved farther up than he'd set it at.

A warm glow flickered through the pickup's back window, and Baker centered himself in the rearview mirror. Flames breached outward from what used to be Marc De Leon's compound. The structure was caving in on itself, lit up by dying fires. "Jocelyn!"

She'd been in the house. She might be hurt, suffering. He wedged one hand against the other and tried to slide the opposite cuff free, but it wouldn't budge. The son of a bitch who'd knocked him out had known exactly what he'd been doing. Baker thrust his upper body forward and licked the skin around the cuff on his right hand. Anything to get the damn thing off.

The Kevlar vest he'd borrowed from Jocelyn hit the steering wheel.

A muted beep issued from somewhere inside the fabric.

Baker's heart threatened to stop.

He pinched his elbows together, trying to get a view down the front of the vest, but it was too dark inside the cabin of the truck. He was still wearing the device. He hadn't gone through a whole lot of bomb training, but he knew any movement on his part—any shift in his weight—could set it off. Giving the bastard who'd ambushed him exactly what he wanted—Baker dead.

A flare burst from the scene behind him, and a thousand tons of grief and rage and loss knotted in the spot where his heart used to reside. He hadn't been there for his sister when she'd needed him the most. He wasn't going to sit here and lose Jocelyn, too.

Baker knew every inch of this truck. The Ghost had most likely stripped out the weapons and obviously had gotten hold of his keys, but the bastard wouldn't have been able to search every hiding place. Baker just had to figure out a way to get to them.

He tried to bring one foot up to leverage against the dashboard, but there was no room between him and the seat. Tugging one hand toward the center console, he jerked his wrist as hard as he dared. But the cuff wouldn't break. There was only one way out of here, and it would come with a lot of pain.

"You can do this." He had to. For Jocelyn. He'd sworn that day in the barn that he would see this through to the end, but he couldn't do that without his partner. No matter how incredibly frustrating her positivity and enthusiasm and outlook on life was, Jocelyn had somehow buried beneath his armor and taken over. They'd survived together. That meant more to him than anything else he'd known with his own deputies. Baker threaded one hand into the smallest opening on the steering wheel, grabbed hold of it with the other and set his head against the faux leather. "You can do this."

Taking a bracing breath, he pulled his wrist against the steering wheel frame with everything he had. The crunch of bone drilled straight through him just before the pain struck. His scream filled the cabin and triggered a high-pitched ringing in his ears. Every muscle in his body tensed to take the pressure off, but it didn't do a bit of good. Baker threw his head back against the headrest. "Damn it!"

The cuff slipped over his hand. Lightning and tears struck behind his eyelids as he drove his broken hand between the driver's side door and seat. The panel came away easily, and he pulled a backup set of truck keys from the hidden space. Along with a handcuff key. Exhaustion and pain closed in fast, demanding he shut down, but Baker wasn't going to stop.

Not until he knew Jocelyn was safe.

He made quick work of the second cuff and shoved the truck key into the ignition. The speedometer wavered in his vision, and he felt himself lean forward as the metric dashboard lit up. He paused just before the engine caught. What were the chances De Leon hadn't rigged the vehicle to blow as a backup plan?

Baker released his hold on the keys and stumbled from the truck. He couldn't risk it. Cacti and several acres of dry, cracked earth were all that stood between him and his partner. He took that first step. The device packed into his vest registered a beep. Then again as he took another step. Every foot he added between him and the truck seemed to anger whatever was packed against his ribs.

He clawed at the Velcro securing him inside the heavy material, but the damn thing wouldn't release. Warning shot through him. His entire nervous system focused on getting out of the too-tight armor while valuable seconds ticked away.

The house was crumbling a mere eighth of a mile away, and he couldn't hear any kind of emergency response echoing through the canyon below. He was all Jocelyn had. His own life be damned.

Baker pumped his legs as fast as they'd allow. His wrist was swelling twice its normal size, but he couldn't think about that. "I'm coming, Joce. Just hang on."

The flames were the only source of light a thousand feet above Alpine Valley. It would be impossible to miss them. Backup was coming. He had to believe that. He shoved through the front gate barely hanging by its hinges and up the now rippled paved path to where the front door used to sit. Jocelyn had been right from the beginning. They'd walked straight into a trap at his insistence, and now she was going to pay the price.

Just as his sister had.

The beeping coming from his vest kept in rhythm with his racing heart rate. Any second now, it would stop, but he'd do whatever it took to find Jocelyn before then.

The floor shook beneath him as the house fought to stay in one piece. Smoke fled up through the new hole in the ceiling, leaving nothing but an emptiness Baker couldn't shake. "Jocelyn!"

He forced himself to slow enough to pick out a response through the crackling flames licking up walls still standing, but he got nothing. He shouldn't have left her. They'd agreed to stick together because they hadn't known what they were walking into, but uncovering the link between Marc De Leon and the Ghost was the first real lead he'd had in months. It'd consumed him and wouldn't let go.

Now he knew the truth. He'd had the man who'd killed Linley within reach all this time.

Baker lunged back as a beam swung free from the ceiling and crashed into its supporting wall two feet ahead. Embers exploded from the impact and sizzled against his skin.

This place was falling apart at the seams, and unless they got out of here right now, they were going down with it. He shook his head to keep himself in the present. "Come on, woman. Where *are* you? Jocelyn!"

Another tremor rolled through the house.

Only this time, it didn't feel like it was from the walls coming down on themselves. Baker backed up a step, staring at the floor. A myriad of cracks spidered across the tiles. Most likely from the impact of the bomb, but his gut said that last quake was from something else. Something far more dangerous.

His vest hadn't given up screaming at him to get back to the truck, but the incessant beeping had become background noise to everything else going on around him. He took another step backward toward where he'd come in, watching one crack spread wider at his feet. The compound sat at the edge of a cliff overlooking Alpine Valley. This place wasn't just coming down on itself…

It was about to slide right into the canyon.

Panic welded to each of his nerve endings. He searched the rubble within arm's reach, then shot forward to clear as many rooms as he could. The living room, dining room, kitchen, patio—

He caught sight of the pool outside, nearly falling in as desperation to find something—anything— that told him Jocelyn was still alive took hold. That he hadn't condemned her to the same fate as his sister. But it was too dark, and the device's beeping had reached an alarming rate. He couldn't do a damn thing for Jocelyn if he suddenly became spaghetti. "The water."

The devices used in the Chief Trevino's murder and at the station had been triggered by pagers. If he could disrupt the signal, he might have a chance. Baker took a deep breath and launched himself into the pool feet first. The Kevlar dragged him straight to the bottom, and it took everything he had to claw back to the surface.

The beeping had stopped. Relief flooded through him. Whatever receiver De Leon had utilized to trigger the device had failed. Latching on to the side of the pool, he hauled himself to the lip. A footprint gleamed from a few feet away. Bare. No more than a size seven or eight. Jocelyn's?

A crack splintered through the cement in front of him.

A resulting groan registered from the ground. The split shot beneath the water, and a frenzy of bubbles escaped to the surface. Every cell in his body ordered him to move. What'd started as a hairline fracture widened until Baker had to swim to keep from getting sucked down into the cyclone forming in the middle of the pool.

Water drained within seconds, and he stabbed his toes into the wall for leverage. Only he wasn't fast enough to get out. Pain splintered through his broken wrist as he tried holding on to the edge with both hands to avoid getting sucked into the black cavern nine feet below. "Jocelyn!"

His fingers weren't strong enough to hold his weight.

And he slipped.

Chapter Eight

She could give up cookies, but she was no quitter.

Jocelyn pumped her legs as hard as she could. Cacti and scrub brush tore at her soaked pants and threatened to bring her down, but she had to get the SUV.

It was the only way to warn Socorro of what was about to happen.

Tremors radiated out from where Marc De Leon's compound used to stand. The entire cliffside was about to slide into the canyon and wipe out Alpine Valley with it. They had to evacuate. She clamped a hand over the wound in her shoulder to distract herself from the pain, but it was no use. The bullet had torn through muscle and tissue and left her with nothing but a craving to numb out. She couldn't. Not now. Not again.

The SUV came into sight as she charged full force along the dirt road that'd once lead to the compound. Her head pounded in rhythm with her shallow breathing. She was almost there. She was going to make it. Jocelyn might not have been able to save her husband from the suffering and agony, but she could save those people down there.

Hitting the lock release on her keys, she slowed as the headlights failed to light up. She'd gone into the water. The mechanism had most likely shorted out. She pushed herself harder. Every second it took to get word back to Socorro was another possible life lost when the cliff crumbled.

"Jocelyn!" Her name tendriled through the focused haze. That voice. She knew that voice. It was enough to stop her short of the SUV and turn back to the flaming remains of the house.

"Baker?" A war raged behind her breastbone. He was alive! Within reach if she retraced her steps, but that need to bury the pain of not being there for her husband at his last moments held her incapacitated. Seconds distorted into frozen minutes as the ground crumbled beneath her feet. The cliff was failing. And it would take Baker with it if she didn't do something. Jocelyn cut her gaze to her SUV. It was right there.

But she didn't have time to warn the people of Alpine Valley and get to Baker, too.

"I'll make the choice easy for you." A fist rocketed into the side of her face. "You don't get to save either."

She hit the ground. The wind was knocked out of her as rock and dirt infiltrated the hole in her shoulder. She tensed against the kick headed for her rib cage. Her attacker's boot ricocheted off her kneecap and sent her body into overdrive. Jocelyn shoved upright with one hand. Hugging her injured arm close, she swung with the other. But missed.

"You're a fighter, aren't you?" The back of the bastard's hand swiped across her face. "Can't even be put down by a bullet. I'm impressed but in a bit of a hurry."

Momentum spun her to one side. Blood bloomed inside her mouth where her teeth cut into the soft tissues of her cheek. It took longer than it should have to recover, but she'd already been running on fumes. Adrenaline would only take her so far.

"Who the hell are you?" She stuggled to keep her balance.

"I've gone by a lot of names. Your chief of police called me a ghost." The dark silhouette with his back to the flames advanced. "But to my friends, I'm simply a craftsman."

The Ghost. The same bomber who'd killed Baker's sister?

"Your friends." She'd trained her body not to shut down in the face of danger, but the numbness was already starting to kick in. It cascaded from her fingers into her chest and blocked her ability to stay in the moment. And without that, she was nothing. "Sangre por Sangre."

"I'm curious. What made you think you'd be enough to take on an organization who pays back any strike tenfold in blood, Jocelyn?" he asked.

He knew her name. Had most likely researched her and her team. Read about her past. "Is that what this is? Payback for a Socorro operative destroying the cartel's headquarters?"

"That's a little above your pay grade." He turned his back on her, heading toward the compound. To finish what he'd started with Baker? "For now, walk away while you still can."

"The cliffside is about to collapse. Hundreds of people are going to die if we don't warn them to evacuate." Piercing pain burned through her side. The stitches. She must've torn them sometime in the last few minutes. Something warm and wet battled with the chill of pool water in her waistband.

"Blood for blood, Jocelyn." The bomber barely angled his head over his shoulder as he strode away from her. "The warning is right there in the name. Go home. You're going to need your strength before I'm finished."

Jocelyn dug her thumb into the bullet wound. Her nerves took care of the rest, sending feeling and another shot of adrenaline through her. She couldn't let any more innocent lives pay for her mistakes. Couldn't let Baker die. The weight would crush her.

"No."

She lunged. Grabbing for the bomber's shoulder, she dropped to both knees as he swung to face her and slammed her good elbow into his gut. He took the impact better than she'd expected. Right before arcing his fist into her face.

The world turned upside down as she landed on her chest. Her ribs couldn't take much more before they snapped. Jocelyn stared up at figure standing above her, and the first real tendril of fear snaked into her brain. She was supposed to be stronger than this.

"You really should've quit while you were ahead."

He reached for her. "Oh, well. I guess I could use you to my advantage after all."

Jocelyn rocketed her bare foot into his ankle with everything she had. His legs swept out from under him, and she rolled to avoid getting pinned beneath his body. His rough exhale was the only evidence she'd delivered any kind of damage, but she didn't have time for victory to take hold. Spinning on her hip, she secured the bastard's head between both thighs, then locked her ankles together. And squeezed. "I think you've done enough damage for one day."

He dug his fingertips into the soft skin of her legs to get free, but it was no use. His strangled sounds barely reached her ears. She was no longer ashamed of the thunder thighs other girls had teased her about in high school. Soon, they would be what saved Alpine Valley.

"You...need me." The bomber tried to pry her knees apart. Then lost consciousness.

Jocelyn unlocked her ankles from around each other and shoved back. He lay motionless on the ground, but the rise and fall of his back said she hadn't killed him. She thrust herself to her feet and ran for the SUV. Stabbing the key into the door lock, she twisted and ripped the door back on its hinges to get to the radio inside. "Socorro, this is Carville. Do you read? Over."

Static infiltrated the sound of her heart thudding hard behind her ears. She pinched the push-to-talk button again. "Socorro, this is Carville. Please respond."

"Jocelyn, what the hell is going on out there?" Jones's voice ratcheted her blood pressure higher. "There was an explosion at the top of the cliff. We need you to run logistics. Fire and Rescue can't get there in time. Where are you?"

She pinched the radio. "I'm already here. Listen, I don't have time to explain. It was a bomb, and the cliff is going to give out any second. We need to get everybody out of Alpine Valley. Now!"

Jocelyn didn't wait for an answer. She'd done what she could to raise the alarm. But Baker was still inside the compound. Tossing the radio, she pulled a set of cuffs from the middle console. The bomber was still there, lying face down in the dirt.

She centered her knee in his lower back and hiked each hand into the cuffs. "You're not going anywhere."

A burst of flame shot up from one side of the compound.

She raced across dry desert as her body threatened to fail. Blood seeped down her leg from the wound in her side, but she wasn't going to stop. Not until she got Baker out of here. Intense heat licked at her exposed skin as she wound through the front gate and back into the collapsing structure.

It was harder to breathe in here. "Baker!"

"Jocelyn?" His voice grew more frantic. Louder. Stronger. "I'm here! In the pool!"

She tried to keep her clothes and hands from brushing against the walls—afraid she'd take down what was left of the structure from contact alone—and cut through what used to be the kitchen.

She froze at the destroyed patio door.

A wide chasm split through where the pool should've been. The water was gone. The chunk of wall that'd pinned her to the bottom of the pool balanced precariously over a mini canyon before falling straight into the darkness. Her mouth dried. Had she been too late? "Baker!"

"Over here!" His voice cut through the panic setting up residence inside her and led her to the edge of the gap splitting the earth in two.

"Just hold on. I'm coming!" The chasm had widened to at least three feet and was growing every second she stood there, but she could make it. She had to. Jocelyn shuffled backward a handful of steps, then launched herself over the unending blackness. Glass and rock cut into the bottoms of her feet as she landed on the other side, but it wasn't enough to slow her down. Reaching the edge of the pool, she thrust her hand down. "Grab onto me!"

Baker's calloused palm grated against hers before it slipped free. He was at the bottom of the pool. Nine feet below her. He had to jump to reach. "You're too high!"

But there was nowhere else for him to go. The shallower the pool, the closer he'd get to the chasm tearing away from the canyon wall. She got down onto her chest, wedging her injured shoulder against the cement. "Come on. You can do it! Try again."

He jumped, securing his hand around hers.

Just as the cliffside gave way.

THE GROUND DISAPPEARED out from under him.

Baker leveraged his toes into the side of the pool, but it was no use. The rough coating merely flecked beneath his weight. He dropped another inch, threatening to take Jocelyn down with him. The pool was gone. Nothing in its place as the earth split in two.

"Hang on!" Her voice barely registered over the ear-deafening sound of destruction as rock, metal and cement gave into gravity. She clamped another hand around his and tried to haul him higher. "I need your other hand!"

He swung his broken wrist toward her, and she latched on. Agonizing pain radiated through his hand and arm. But his scream didn't compare to the compound slipping into the protective canyon around Alpine Valley.

Jocelyn somehow managed to drag him upward, high enough for him to get one foot over the edge of the pool. "Almost there."

Gravel and glass pressed into his temple as he collapsed face-first. Dust drove into his lungs. He fought for breath, but it was useless against the overwhelming tide of grief swallowing him whole. Staring out at the new ridge overlooking the town he loved, he willed the people below to survive. Though didn't know how they would.

"We were too late," he said.

Another tremor rumbled beneath them, and Marc De Leon's compound sank another foot into the ground. The entire structure leaned at an impossible angle, hiking Baker's nervous system into overdrive.

"We have to get out of here." Jocelyn shoved back from the edge of the pool with her hands and feet. No trace of enthusiasm or lightness in her expression, and he needed that slice of inner light. Just a fraction to counter the ramifications of Alpine Valley being crushed by thousands of tons of rock.

Dust kicked up and threatened to choke them both as they launched over the half wall blocking off the backyard from the house itself. Quakes seemed to follow their every step as they maneuvered around the perimeter of the compound. A gut-wrenching tremor divided the front of the house away from the back. The ground lurched beneath them, and Jocelyn fell into him.

"I've got you." He kept her upright as best he could while trying to stay on his own two feet. The chasm that'd split the pool in half had grown. There was no way to jump it, but they still had a way out. "We have to go over the wall. I'll give you a boost."

She didn't wait for an explanation as he bent down to clasp her foot. Blood stained his hand as he hiked her against the wall. Jocelyn turned back for him from the top, offering one hand. "Watch out!"

The ground shifted, knocking him off his feet. The cavity cutting through the backyard was inching toward him.

They were out of time.

Baker fought against the weight of the Kevlar vest packed with explosive and lurched upward. He caught Jocelyn's forearm, and together, they hauled his weight over the wall. But they couldn't celebrate yet. The crack in the earth was spreading. Darting right toward them.

They rolled off the top of the wall as one. Only Jocelyn didn't land on her feet. The thud of her body registered harder than it should have.

"Come on, Carville. We've got to move. This place is coming apart at the seams."

"I think I broke something." Her voice tried to hide the pain she must've been feeling, but he didn't miss it. Something was seriously wrong. Hell, she'd already survived two explosions. How much more could he possibly ask of her?

"Hang on to me." Out of breath, Baker threaded his broken wrist beneath her knees and dragged her away from the barrier crumbling two feet away. Meant to be a protective guard between the compound and the outside world, every stone was swallowed as the cliff broke away from the canyon wall.

The last remnants of the compound slipped over the edge as Baker collapsed with Jocelyn in his arms. The bomb had destroyed more than a single home. There had to be hundreds buried under rubble and dirt below. His heart strained to rip out of his chest as he considered the loss of life of the very people he'd sworn to protect. "It's gone. All of it…is gone."

"I'm sorry. I tried to warn them." Jocelyn framed one hand against his face. Cold and rough. Nothing like when she'd kissed him. Her voice wavered. "I… radioed my team…"

Her hand fell away, and every muscle in her body went slack.

"Joce?" He scanned her face in the bright moonlight. Then realized she was no longer wearing her vest. And noticed the blood. Wet, glimmering against her clothing. Oh, hell. The echo of a gunshot in his head rendered him frozen for a series of breaths.

Baker laid her across the desert floor, ripping at her T-shirt. There was a hole in her shoulder. She'd taken a bullet but somehow still managed to get him out of the compound in one piece. How was that *possible*? And where the hell was Maverick when Baker needed him? "Talk to me, Goose."

He couldn't think about all those lives down there in Alpine Valley with Jocelyn needing him right now. Struggling to his feet, he hauled her against his chest and started walking toward the SUV. Her added weight wiped his strength from him, and Baker collapsed to one knee.

Two bombs. Losing a fight to a cartel bomber. A device strapped to his chest. And now an apocalyptic event that'd destroyed everything he had left. All within twenty-four hours. He wasn't sure he could take much more, but he wouldn't leave Jocelyn out here to fend for herself. She'd saved his life. The least he could do was return the favor.

Baker bit back a groan when pain singed through his nerve endings as he regained his footing. A hundred feet. That was all he had left before they reached the SUV. They were going to make it. They had to. Because they'd survived too damn much to give up now. "We've got this."

But every step seemed to put them farther away

from the vehicle. Or maybe his mind had finally started shutting down from all the explosions going on around them. His clothing suctioned to him with Jocelyn's body heat furnaced against him. "Just a little farther."

He stepped on something that didn't belong. Metallic and light. Too far from the blast area. Maneuvering his partner out of the way, Baker made out a pair of cuffs lying there in the dirt. Open. Warning triggered at the base of his spine, as though he were being watched. Marc De Leon had left Baker for dead inside his own truck, but even though the son of a bitch's plan failed, that didn't mean this was over.

He set sights on Jocelyn's SUV. He couldn't trust his own instincts right then, but something was telling him getting in that vehicle would be the end of them both. Emergency crews would have their hands tied trying to dig residents out of the landslide. The SUV was the only way to get Jocelyn help in time. Baker took another step toward the SUV.

The explosion lit up the sky.

Heat licked over his skin and knocked him back on his ass. His head snapped back and hit the ground harder than he expected. Blinding pain became his entire world right then, and Jocelyn slipped out of his hold. It took too long for his senses to get back in the game despite his desperation to keep moving.

The threat wasn't over. He had to get up. Had to keep fighting.

Baker risked prying his eyelids open. The crackle of flames was too bright, too loud. His brain was having a hard time processing each individual sound, mixing it up with the pop and crack of those that'd burned down his life.

Jocelyn's hand moved to touch his between them, a simple brush of skin-to-skin. The past threatened to consume him from the inside. He felt as though he were about to leave his body, but the grounding feel of her kept him in one place.

Light reflected off her dark pupils as she set sights on him. The smile he'd once resented tugged at her mouth. "I've…got you. Always."

Adrenaline drained from his veins and brought down his heart rate as black webs spidered in his peripheral vision. Baker secured his hand around hers, and the constant readiness and vibrations running through him quieted for the first time in years. Because of her. "I've got you, too, partner."

Bouncing bright lights registered from over Jocelyn's shoulder. Flashlights? Baker couldn't be sure as he tried to force his body to move, but none of his brain's commands were being carried out. He'd given his fight-or-flight response permission to take a break, and now it would take a miracle to come back online. He gripped Jocelyn's hand harder. Then again, he was starting to believe in miracles. "I want an entire tray of cookies after this."

"Done." Her smile weakened as she slipped back into unconsciousness.

Heavy footsteps pounded against the desert floor. Closing in fast. Baker rolled to one side, ready to protect the woman who'd nearly given her life for him.

It took every ounce of strength he possessed to get to his feet. Then he raised his fists. He'd take on the entire cartel if it meant getting Jocelyn out of this alive. The bouncing flashlights merged into one. His brain was playing tricks on him, but he wasn't going to back down.

"Chief, is that you?" Jones Driscoll slowed his approach, a flashlight in one hand and a weapon in the other. Utter disbelief contorted the man's expression. Hell, Baker must've looked a lot worse than he'd thought.

The combat controller holstered his weapon and pressed his hand between Jocelyn's shoulder blades. "She's still breathing. Damn. You two sure know how to throw a party. What happened out here?"

"You mean apart from the fact a Sangre por Sangre bomber just destroyed an entire town in a landslide?" Baker stumbled back as the fight left him in a rush. His knees bit into the ground beside Jocelyn. "She saved my life."

Chapter Nine

Today would be a cookie dough day.

Because the beeping was back. The sound she hated more than Maverick's howls in the middle of the night. She was back in a hospital. Jocelyn lifted one hand, though something kept her from extending her fingers completely. She fought the grogginess of whatever pain medication the staff had put her on. Her breathing came easier when she couldn't feel, but it wasn't permanent. It couldn't be.

A low growl vibrated through her leg. Then something familiar. A metallic ping of ID tags. She turned her hand upward, fisting a handful of fur. "Maverick."

He was here. And pinning her to the bed with his massive weight. The German shepherd licked at her wrist before laying his head back down, and Jocelyn summoned the courage to force her eyes open. Only this time there were no bright fluorescent lights or bleached white tile to blind her.

She wasn't in a hospital.

Instead, black flooring with matching black cabinets encircled the private room. Socorro's medical wing. The overhead lights had been dimmed, and the beeping, she just realized, was definitely not as loud as it could've been.

"Thought you could use some time together after what happened." Baker's voice pulled her attention from her K-9 partner to the man at her left. Dark bruising rorschached beneath one eye and across his temple. There were other markers too—cuts and scrapes that evidenced what they'd been through. Though the splint around his wrist was the most telling of them all.

Jocelyn didn't have the will or the energy to try to sit up. "How long have you been sitting there watching me sleep?"

"About six hours." Baker got up from his chair positioned a couple feet from the side of the bed. "Dr. Piel—is that her name?—patched me up nicely, and hey, no waiting to get looked at. I think I might switch providers. Do you know if she takes my insurance?"

"I'm afraid she only sees private patients." Her laugh lodged halfway up her throat, stuck in the dryness brought on by aerosolized dirt and debris and ash. But there wasn't any pain—which, now that she thought about it, shouldn't have been possible.

Not as long as she'd been given the right pain-killer.

Jocelyn followed the IV line from the back of her hand to the clear baggy bulging with liquid above her. Morphine. Dr. Piel wouldn't have known. Nobody in this building knew. She moved to disconnect the line from the catheter, but the moment she pulled it free, the pain would come back.

Maverick lifted his head, watching her every move. Not unlike Baker. He was intelligent, focused and observational. No one in their right mind would choose to go through unending waves of pain after what they'd been through rather than numb out with painkiller. Weaning herself off the meds now would only raise suspicion. And she couldn't deal with that right now.

"You okay?" Concern etched deep into the corners of Baker's mouth. "Do you need me to get the doctor?"

"I'm...fine." She tried recalling the events leading up to her arrival back at headquarters, but there were too many missing fragments. "Tell me what happened."

"Well, your warning worked." He moved to the side of the bed, sliding one hand over her wrapped ankle. The thin gauze around the joint said she hadn't broken it as she believed. More likely a hard sprain. "Socorro was able to evacuate nearly everyone who might be impacted by the landslide. Though that didn't stop the canyon wall from caving in. You saved a lot of lives, Joce. Without you, Alpine Valley would be in rough shape. Well, rougher shape."

Joce. He hadn't called her that before. It made her want to believe they were more than two people thrust together in the aftermath of a bombing, but her heart hurt at the idea. Of tying herself to someone else. Because when that tie broke—as they inevitably did—she would be right back in the dark hole she'd spent so long trying to climb out of. Just like she'd done after Miles's death. Her stomach twisted into one overextended knot. "Were there any casualties?"

"Not a single one." He shook his head, a hint of wonder in his voice. "You and your team, as much as I hate to admit it, really saved our bacon. Thank you, Jocelyn. For everything. If I hadn't rushed to find Marc De Leon, maybe none of this would've happened, and I'm so sorry for that."

"He killed your sister, didn't he?" she asked.

"Yeah. He did." Baker scrubbed a hand down his face, a habit he'd picked up on whenever he wanted to avoid a tough topic. It was a defense mechanism. Avoid the question to avoid the feelings that came with it, but it didn't make the hard things go away. At least, not in her experience. "I thought we would find De Leon and get him to identify the Ghost, but the explosive he packed into my Kevlar vest turned out to be the same blueprint for those used to kill Jane Doe three months ago. I had him, Jocelyn. All this time. I just didn't connect the dots."

Jocelyn bit back the urge to remind him of her warning before they'd gone into that house. A Sangre por Sangre lieutenant's compound had been attacked. The cartel would only take the event as an act of war. Sooner or later, they'd learn Alpine Valley's chief of police and a Socorro operative had been there, and then... The crap would really hit the fan. It was only a matter of time. "But?"

"I was so sure of myself, going in there." He shook his head again, much more aggressively as though to dislodge the theory altogether. "But something is

off. The man we fought... He told me I didn't have
to watch my sister die right in front of me, that I was
spared that horror as she burned. Made it seem like
he'd gone through all that himself. That he'd lost
someone, too."

"Cartels like Sangre por Sangre experience in-
fighting all the time. Hostile takeovers, executions
for not following orders. Dozens of people have died
in their attempts to claw to the top of the ladder."
Her heart hurt. Which didn't make sense because
the morphine was supposed to numb her from her
scalp to her toes.

Jocelyn fisted her hand back into Maverick's fur.
She needed to get out of here. To not be forced to stay
still. To get her hands in some dough. "Or maybe,
after everything you've been through, you want what
he said to be true. Maybe, after all this time, you've
been looking for someone who's been through the
same thing you have."

"You could be right. Maybe everything he said
out there was just another way to mess with my head.
Unfortunately, Marc De Leon is in the wind. Nobody, not even his attorney, has been able to get a
hold of him. The prosecutor is trying to go through
the cartel, but it's looking like we've hit a dead end."
He blew out a frustrated breath. "So far, he's managed to detonate three bombs without leaving much
of a trace. From what I can tell, he was planning
on blowing me up just like he blew up Ponderosa's
chief of police."

Baker took up position at the side of the bed, the

mattress dipping beneath his weight and triggering a low growl from Maverick. "Cool it, Cujo. I got you out of your crate."

She scratched behind Maverick's ear. As much as it'd annoyed her in the minutes leading up to the explosion at the station, she found Baker's nicknames for the German shepherd the exact kick to get her out of the spiral closing in. "One of these days, he's going to make you wish you'd called him by his real name."

"One of these days?" Surprise glimmered in Baker's dark eyes and tendriled through the numbness circulating through her body. Hard to imagine a man like Baker being surprised by anything, but she'd somehow managed. "Does that mean you're not tapping out of this investigation?"

Jocelyn pressed her shoulders into the pillow to distract herself from the unpleasant thoughts waiting for a clear path through her mind. She'd fought them off this long. She could do it a while longer. She just had to concentrate and paste another smile on her face. "Hey, that guy blew me up, too, remember? I have as much a personal stake in this as you do."

"How do you do it, Jocelyn?" His voice dipped into a near whisper. "How can you stay so positive after everything that's happened?"

It was his turn to walk straight past the barriers she housed herself inside. Pinching the hem of the thin white sheet beneath her thumbnail, she sifted through a thousand answers in search of the one that would change the subject as quickly as possible. But her threshold for pain, for loss, for defensiveness had been reached long before they'd walked into Marc De Leon's compound. "It takes a lot of effort. A lot of forcing myself to look for silver linings on stormy days."

"Then why do it?" he asked.

"Because if I don't, I'm afraid of who I'll become." She'd been on the morphine too long. It was inhibiting her internal filter. "I'll go back to who I used to be. Hollow. Terrified of feeling anything real. I'll shut down, and without the sarcasm and baked goods, movie nights, Christmas parties and trying to bring the team together, I'm afraid they're going to realize I don't have anything to offer. No reason to keep me around, and I want to stay, Baker. I need to be part of the team. Socorro's team. Otherwise, I'll go back to..."

No. She couldn't. She couldn't give up that piece of herself. Not to him. Not to any of them. Nothing good had come of it before.

"Back to what?" Yet even as he spoke the words, he seemed to accept she wasn't going to answer that question. Baker interlaced his fingers with hers. A vicious scrape had scabbed over between his thumb and forefinger, arousing the nerves in her hand. "You run logistics for your entire team. You made sure soldiers got what they needed overseas. You fight for towns like Alpine Valley to get the resources they need in a crisis. I've seen it. You're vital to this operation." He swallowed hard. "If it wasn't for you, I'd be dead right now and half the people of this town would be buried under a landslide. Whatever you're afraid of, you're stronger than you think you are."

She wanted to believe him, with every ounce of

her being, she wanted what he said to be true. But that alone didn't make it reality. Jocelyn watched as another drop of pain medication infiltrated her IV line. "That was before."

His thumb skimmed over the top of her hand. "Before what?"

Closing her eyes, she lost the battle raging inside and let her eyes slip closed. "Before all I cared about was being numb."

JOCELYN HAD BEEN cleared to recover in her room.

Mid-morning sunlight infiltrated through the floor-to-ceiling window at his back and cast his shadow across Socorro's dining room table. Baker wasn't sure how long he'd stared at his own outline, willing his brain to produce something—anything— that would give him a clue as to where Marc De Leon had gone. And his motive for wanting him dead.

He replayed the bastard's words in his head too many times to count, until he wasn't sure which thoughts had been his own and which had belonged to the bomber. Baker leafed through Albuquerque's scene report from the initial bombing at the station. Nitroglycerin packed into a pipe bomb. De Leon obviously didn't care about the impact of his chemicals on the environment, but Baker couldn't actually name a cartel soldier who did. Newspaper dated over the past two weeks had been used as filler, but pulling fingerprints had been impossible.

The bomber had been careful. Most likely worn gloves. A brand-new car battery had been used to

spark the initial charge, and the device had been triggered by a pager. In line with the other sixteen incidents accredited to the Ghost, including the bombing
on Baker's property. Though he was looking at another dead end there. The company who'd manufac-
tured this one had gone out of business years ago. A
relic. No way to trace the purchase, and the number
of the damn thing was registered to an unending list
of dummy corporations. "Why trust an old piece of
technology when you could get your hands on something guaranteed to go off?"

Why take the risk? Baker had been asking himself the same question for over two hours in front
of a dozen crime scene photos scattered all over the
dining room table. He'd helped himself to one of
the prepared meals Jocelyn was known for—this
one lasagna and a heavy helping of garlic bread and
a citrus salad he hadn't touched yet. But no matter
how much food he packed into his stomach or how
many minutes he sat there with his eyes closed, the
answer refused to surface.

The trill of dog tags cut through the headache
building at the base of his skull. He was running on
fumes, and he knew it. Awake for more than twenty-
four hours. Hell, he shouldn't have been able to walk,
but this was important. Cutting his attention to the
German shepherd perched to one side, Baker bit back
his annoyance. Maverick had followed him from Jocelyn's room. Though he couldn't think of a reason
other than Baker had access to her food. "Are you
allowed to eat from the table?"

Maverick cocked his head to one side and licked his lips. The K-9 really was something now that Baker got a look at him. Lean, healthy, warm brown eyes. It was any wonder Jocelyn had fallen in love with him, but how they'd ended up together was as big a mystery as why Marc De Leon had blown up his own compound.

Jocelyn worked logistics for the military. No reason for her to come in contact with explosive ordinance on tour. Which made Baker think they'd met through some other means.

"You protect her, though. That's why you nearly bit my hand off at the station."

Maverick pawed at the floor.

"You want to bite my hand off right now, don't you?" Baker collected his fork and took a stab at a section of lasagna, then offered it to the dog.

The shepherd licked the entire fork clean. Overhead lighting caught on the mutt's ID tags, and Baker got his first real look at them. "Those aren't military tags."

Maneuvering his legs out from under the table, he stretched his hand out. A warning signaled in Maverick's chest, and Baker stilled. No show of teeth, though. That was something.

"I'm not going to hurt you. Just want to look at your tags," he said. "I promise to stop calling you Cujo if you promise not to bite me while I do that. Deal?"

He inched forward again, slower this time. His fingers brushed against course black and brown fur at Maverick's neck, and the shepherd closed his eyes in exhilaration. The dog's tongue made an appearance as Baker targeted the area he'd noticed Jocelyn scratching in the med unit. "There. See? We're friends. You like that?"

He kept up the scratching with one hand and brought the other to the tags to read the stamped lettering: "Maverick. Federal Protective Service. Miles Carville."

An invisible sucker punch emptied the air out of his chest. More effective than any bomb he'd survived thus far. "Your mama wasn't the only one who lost someone, was she?"

Maverick's whine almost convinced Baker the dog had understood him. It made sense now. Jocelyn's husband had worked for the Department of Homeland Security, and when he'd died, Maverick would've been forced to retire, too. The relationship between handler and K-9 took years to cultivate, from the time the German shepherd would've been a puppy. Maverick wouldn't have responded to anyone else and ultimately would've become useless for the team once Miles Carville had died. But Jocelyn had kept him, literally kept a piece of her husband that followed her into the field and slept in her room at night. That protected her when it counted. "Damn, dog. I think I might be jealous of you."

"That's possibly the weirdest sentence I've ever heard in my life." Jocelyn leaned against the wide entryway into the kitchen, and hell, she was a sight for sore eyes. A few visible cuts here and there, but nothing that could take away that inner brightness that'd gotten him through the past day and a half.

His gut clenched at how much pain she must've been in. "You're supposed to be resting."

"Girl's gotta eat, doesn't she?" She limped into the dining room and dragged the chair beside his out from beneath the table with her good arm, then took a seat. "Besides, it's hard to sleep when you know the bomber you arrested in the middle of the desert got away. You find anything in Albuquerque's report that might give us an idea of where De Leon might've gone?"

Maverick moved in to be at Jocelyn's side, marking his territory. Funny—Baker felt inclined to do the same. To erase all the times he'd been such an ass to her over the past few months and give her a reason to feel again.

"Not a single clue." They were back at square one. "Bomb was pretty simple. Nitroglycerin explosive, a fresh car battery to initiate the spark, but there's one thing that doesn't make sense."

She reached over the crime scene photos and grabbed for what was left of Baker's dinner. "What's that?"

"The receiver was an old pager," he said.

Three distinct lines deepened between her brows as she sat a bit straighter. Warm brown eyes, almost the same color as Maverick's caramel irises, scanned the photos he'd set across the table. Setting down the fork, she picked up one image in particular. A photo of a motherboard. No transmitter on the once leprechaun-green chip. Just a receiver.

"You're right, but it fits with the Ghost's preferences," she said. "Harder to trace, maybe? Was the bomb squad able to recover a registered number?"

"Not yet." It was easy to look at her and see the

wheels turning. To know she was taking that incredible amount of knowledge she'd gleaned throughout her life to try to figure out why De Leon wanted him dead. Why after all this time, the Ghost had come back to haunt him.

Baker couldn't help but smile as she silently read something to herself. Despite her claim to have as much at stake in this game as he did, that simply wasn't true. She was here for him, and thank heaven for that. Otherwise he'd be at the bottom of that landslide or burned to the driver's seat of his truck. "They're still working through—"

"Let me guess. Dozens of shell companies." Leaning back in her seat, she took a bite of lasagna. Hints of exhaustion still clung beneath her eyes and in her slowed movements. Every shift in her body seemed to aggravate the corners of her mouth, but she wouldn't admit it. She'd never want him to know she was in pain, but not just that. There was something else she wasn't telling him, something she'd held back in the medical suite. Because she still didn't trust him. "I'm starting to feel like I've been here before."

"Chief Trevino's murder." Baker lost the air in his lungs. "Yeah. I had the same thought. By the way, Maverick licked that fork."

Jocelyn let the silverware hit the table. The metallic ping put a dent where it'd landed on the pristine wood, and understanding hit. There were no other dings in the table because nobody used it. All this time, he'd assumed Jocelyn's efforts to bond the team over Christmas breakfasts, birthday parties and family dinners had succeeded.

But the table said otherwise. She'd said she needed to be part of the team. Socorro's team. That she was afraid they'd have no use for her. Because nobody cared as much as she did. No one else made the effort like she did. She needed her team. Needed friends. A physical connection to this world.

"In that case, enjoy the rest of your food." She pressed away from the table, her long, ebony hair sliding against her back. "I'm going to get something from the fridge."

He'd never seen her like this before. The sight was surreal, as though he was witnessing the real her. Not what she wanted everyone to see. Not the logistics coordinator or the former solider. Just Jocelyn. Or, hell, maybe he'd hit his head a lot harder than he'd thought.

Baker tracked her into the kitchen, keeping his feet moving to close the distance between them.

"Don't say anything about how a dog's mouth is cleaner than mine." She wrenched open the refrigerator door between them and pulled a large metal bowl covered in plastic wrap, identical to the one he noted earlier, from inside. Discarding the wrap, she set the bowl on the counter and threw open a drawer to her left. She drove a spoon straight into what looked like a giant bowl of cookie dough. "I don't lick my own butt or chew on my feet."

"Good to know," he said.

She shoved an entire spoonful into her mouth and

seemed to sink back against the counter, completely at ease and absolutely beautiful.

Baker shut the refrigerator door and took the spoon from her hand.

Just before he crushed his mouth to hers.

Chapter Ten

A balanced diet consisted of a cookie in each hand. Or in her case a spoonful of dough.

But having Baker pressed against her was pretty damn fulfilling, too.

Her chest felt like it might burst open, and Jocelyn did the only thing she could think to do. She gave up her hold on the spoon. Sugar, butter, flour and a hint of peppermint spread across her tongue, but this wasn't the gross kind of peppermint. It was Baker. Kissing her. Deep and hard.

And she kissed him back. With every ounce of herself she had left. Because she felt something. As though she could breathe easier, like there was a life outside of her trying to force friendships and combating danger, secrets and grief. Despite all his sharp edges and barbed words, Baker's mouth was soft and determined and capable of washing the violence and fear out of her, leaving her utterly and completely defenseless against the past.

His hand found her waist, just shy of the wound in her side. He was being careful with her, didn't want to cause her any pain, but life never guaranteed there wouldn't be pain. Just that it had to be worth living.

Baker eased his mouth from hers, rolling his lips between his teeth. "Is that the cranberry-lemon dough you've been trying to get me to try?"

"Yeah." Her breath shuddered out of her. Uncontrollable and freeing. She'd only kissed one other man in her life. She and Miles had been high school sweethearts, marrying straight out of basic training before he'd gone to work for the Department of Homeland Security. He had always been able to knock her for a loop, but this… This was something she hadn't expected. Easy. And she desperately wanted easy. Free of fear and grief and expectation.

"It's really good," Baker said.

Jocelyn worked to swallow the taste of him, to make him part of her. The effect cleansed her from the inside, burning through her and sweeping the last claws of the past from her heart. She'd loved her husband. Deeply. And she should've been there at his last moments. But punishing herself day after day didn't honor him. That wasn't the kind of legacy he deserved. "It's even better when it's baked."

"Not sure it could get much better." Baker pressed his mouth to hers a second time, resurrecting sensations she'd forgotten existed. His hands threaded into her hair as though they both might fall apart right there in the middle of the kitchen if he didn't.

A profound shift triggered inside of her, reminding her she was more than a grieving widow, more than an operator for the world's best military contractor. More than her mistakes and flaws. Baker Halsey reminded her she was a woman. One who still had a lot of living to do. Here. In Alpine Valley. "You have no idea what I'm capable of."

A laugh rumbled through his chest and set her squarely back in the present. They'd just made out in Socorro's kitchen, in plain view of anyone who might've walked by. Jocelyn pressed her fingertips to her mouth to keep the smile off her face, but the effort proved in vain.

"Are you going to run away again?" Baker added a few inches of distance between them. "You know, like after I touched you."

"What? No." Her brain scrambled for the words to describe what she'd felt when he'd kissed her, but she was still wrapped up in the heat sliding through her. "This… Things are different between us now than they were then. And that kiss…" Jocelyn scanned the hallway just outside the dual-entrance kitchen. "It was not unpleasant, sir."

"Oh, good. 'Cause I'm a little out of practice. Other than when you kissed me back at the station." The tension in his shoulders drained, and right then she couldn't help but think another invisible scale of his armor was shedding before her eyes. "I didn't hurt you, did I?"

The reminder shot awareness into the wounds and threatened to break whatever this spell was between them, but she didn't feel any pain. There was still a hint of morphine left in her body that would take a few hours to burn off. Blissful numbness that only Baker seemed to penetrate.

The thought pulled her up short. She'd lost her ability to feel because of the loss of one man and had sworn never to go back to that shell of a life. What would happen if she lost another?

Jocelyn forced herself to step back to give her brain a chance to catch up. It was the painkiller throwing the promises she'd made herself out the window. It'd stripped her of her internal fight, but she couldn't lose herself now. Not with a bomber on the loose. "Has Albuquerque PD recovered anything from the land-slide?"

They'd been so caught up in trying to locate Marc De Leon, she'd let her focus be pulled in a thousand different directions. The cartel lieutenant had been charged with murder by Alpine Valley PD. The bomb planted in the station had destroyed any evidence the prosecutor could leverage against him. Though it was starting to look like De Leon was working his own agenda, they couldn't overlook a direct tie to Sangre por Sangre.

"Not yet. I've got my deputies trying to help when they can, but that's hard when they're stuck working out of the rec center. Seems those volleyball players aren't as nice as they look when it comes to sharing the building." Baker slid his hands into his jeans, and it was only then she realized he'd changed out of his uniform. So this was what he looked like out-side of his job.

A laugh escaped. But this time it wasn't forced. It

took her a few seconds to comprehend that unremark-able detail. Everything about her had been forced over the past two years…everything but this. "I guess it's a good thing you're stuck here with me, then."

The humor drained from his expression. "I'm not stuck, Jocelyn. I'm choosing to be here. With you. Because you're a good partner, and you deserve to have a team that supports you. Not out of obligation, but because they want to."

"What makes you think I wouldn't get that from Socorro?" If she had a tell, it would be all over her face right then. Uncomfortable pressure lit up in-side her chest to the point she wasn't sure if her next breath would come without physical orders.

"The dining table." Three words that didn't make sense on their own but drilled through her harder and faster than the pain she'd run from. Baker reached for her, and an engrained shift had her accepting that touch. Needing it more than she'd needed anything ever before. "You talk about brunches and birthday parties. Thanksgiving and dinners together. Movie nights and all those types of things. But there isn't a single scratch or ding in that table except the one you just put there a few minutes ago."

Her mind raced for memories of Cash, Jones, Scarlett, Granger, even Ivy, having her back. "We're military. We watch after each other. No matter what."

"But which one of them would talk to you about your husband, Jocelyn? Which one of them would jump into the fray with you if the bullets weren't flying?" he asked.

And she didn't have an answer.

"I know you're hurting more than you let on. I know what lengths you have to go to to find the silver lining in all of this, but did you ever consider all you're doing is constantly escaping?" His words punctuated with experience she didn't want to recognize. They weren't the same. They hadn't been through the same experiences, but there was a line of connectedness she felt with him. A shared loss that linked them more than she'd ever expected. "Sooner or later, your positivity isn't going to be enough. Your mind and your body are going to force you to process everything you're running from, and you're going to need someone to be there for you."

Truth hit her center mass. He was right. She knew it, and maybe her desperation to bring the team together had been out of some kind of preparation for what waited on the horizon, but it wouldn't be today. Today they had a bomber to find.

Jocelyn straightened a bump in his T-shirt collar with her uninjured hand. "And here I thought you were nothing but a grumpy cop who'd rather save the world alone rather than trust anyone again."

His smile cracked through the intensity of the moment. "Yeah. Well, I guess you surprised me, too."

"Thank you. For having my back out there." She slid her palm over his heart. "And in here."

"You got it, Goose." His gaze locked onto her, and it took her a few moments to remember what it felt like to be fully grounded in the moment. To feel Baker's pulse beneath her hand, his warmth and strength. It was almost enough to bury the shame of the past. Almost.

"Not sure if you know this," she said, "but most women don't like nicknames that relate to overly loud pests of the sky."

"You can't expect Maverick to fly without his wingman." He motioned to the shepherd currently serving himself the rest of Baker's lasagna on his hind legs.

She was going to regret letting him have cheese. "Isn't Goose the one who dies?"

"Yeah, well. Eventually." He was trying to backtrack, and Jocelyn was going to let him keep digging that hole just to watch him squirm. It was endearing and human. Like a reward for all of her hard work to break through that tough shell over the past few months. "But they had a good run."

"If you two are done feeling each other up, we've got a problem." Jones Driscoll rounded into the kitchen, a tablet clutched between both hands. The scar running through his left eyebrow dipped lower as he scanned the screen. "Albuquerque's bomb squad is in the middle of going through what they can dig out of the landslide and what's left of your SUV. So far, they're convinced all three bombs were designed and detonated by the same bomber."

And just like that, they were thrust back into reality. Jocelyn severed her physical connection from Baker. "I'm wondering if you know what *problem* means, Jones?"

"They found a body," the combat controller said.

Baker cut his attention to Jocelyn, and her entire body lit up at the hundreds of possibilities of who else had gotten caught up in this mess. "There wasn't anyone else at the scene. We searched the entire compound."

Jones handed off the tablet. "Then you missed someone."

Jocelyn scanned through the report, horrified as a positive ID matched the burnt remains photographed at the scene. "Marc De Leon. I don't understand. He was the bomber. Why would he go back into the house?"

"He didn't. The coroner is examining the remains as we speak." Jones swiped the screen to bring their attention to a close-up of the body. "According to her, Marc De Leon was dead at least four hours before the bomb detonated."

Baker slumped against the counter. "Then who the hell is trying to kill us?"

IT WASN'T POSSIBLE. He'd been face-to-face with De Leon. He'd talked with the son of a bitch.

But there was no arguing with forensics. Baker had scoured through sixteen bombing reports a dozen times. Didn't change a damn thing. The man he'd wanted for his sister's murder was already dead.

He swiped steam from the mirror. No amount of hot water and soap had cleaned the gritty feel of ash and dirt on his skin, but it'd somehow managed to calm him enough to start thinking clearly.

What the hell had he been thinking to sign up for this job? To believe he could make a difference in people's lives? That he could protect the very town that'd welcome him as one of their own? He didn't have any prior experience. He'd never been through the police academy or basic training. Hell, he'd had to teach himself how to hold and fire a weapon from the internet, a secret that would die with him. He'd taken the chief of police position mere weeks after Sangre por Sangre had burned everything he'd loved to the ground, and the world had been so black and white. All he'd had was a promise. To protect Alpine Valley when no one else was stepping up to the plate.

But now… He wasn't the man for this job. And revenge wasn't enough anymore. Cartel raids, two-faced deputies, dead bodies, bombs going off everywhere he stepped—it combined into an undeniable sense of failure. He hadn't been able to stop any of it. And now the only light he'd found at the end of the tunnel had been snuffed out. He'd stepped into the middle of a war that had no end. Day after day, Sangre por Sangre and organizations like it were gaining power all across New Mexico—this place he loved more than his childhood home.

Who was he to stand up against a monster like that?

Memories infiltrated the hollowness pressing in on him from every angle. Linley smiling over her shoulder as she took her first ride around the horse ring. He'd never seen her smile like that. Never seen her so damn happy. He'd known then they'd never be able to walk away from the dream they'd built together. That they'd each found what they'd been looking for. In each other, and here, in Alpine Valley.

But it wasn't enough. Not anymore.

Baker made quick work of drying off and changing into a fresh set of sweats one of Jocelyn's teammates had lent him. The T-shirt was a bit too big, though, to the point that he looked like a toddler dressing up in his daddy's clothes. So he tugged it off, mindful of the aches and pains in his torso as he reentered Jocelyn's bedroom.

The space wasn't much bigger than a hotel room, and the dim lighting within it failed to compete with a massive bay windows that looked straight over the tail end of Alpine Valley. The sun had crept into the western half of the sky. The landslide was hidden at this angle, saving him a small amount of torment, but sooner or later, he'd have to face his failure.

Fire and Rescue, the bomb squad and his deputies were going through the rubble. Part of him wanted to be there with them, getting his hands dirty, searching for anyone who hadn't been able to evacuate. But the other part understood the sooner they found the bomber, the sooner this nightmare would end.

"It's not your fault." Jocelyn's voice slipped from the shadows and surrounded him as though she'd physically secured him against her. Warm, soft, accepting. "What happened up on that cliff. Neither of us could've stopped it."

Baker let his gaze settle on the scrap of land that had once held his entire future. "You and I both know we can tell ourselves we aren't at fault. Doesn't make it true."

"That goes both ways, Baker." She took up position beside him, the backside of her hand brushing against his. "We lie to ourselves just as easily."

She had a point.

"I don't know where to go from here." The longer he stared through the window, the less his eyes picked up the small differences of his property. Until he lost sight of the house altogether. "I was so sure I could protect this town, that I could stop the cartel from doing to someone else what they did to me, but I'm just one man. I've got two deputies heading for retirement, one six feet under from collaborating with the cartel, no police station, no dispatcher and a quarter of Alpine Valley under mud, rock and metal."

His laugh wasn't meant to cut through the tension cresting along his shoulders. It was a manifestation of the ridiculousness of that statement. He was supposed to be running a bed and breakfast with his sister, corralling horses, leading tour groups and making the stack of recipes he'd grown up on. And now he'd actually partnered with the very people he blamed for adding fuel to the cartel flames.

Baker half turned toward her. "This is where you tell me to look at the positives and list them out. Because that's the only way I see a way out of this."

"I don't think I can do that." Her voice seemed to scratch up her throat. "Truth is, the longer I'm with you, the more I realize my positivity has been nothing but toxic. For my team, for the people down there relying on us, for Maverick, even. I told myself if I could just focus on the good things going on in my life, they would be enough to drown out the bad, but partnering with you… I don't want to pretend anymore. But at the same time, you're right. There isn't anybody here who would talk to me about my husband, about what it felt like to lose him."

"You haven't told any of them." He wasn't sure where the thought had come from, but he knew it to be truth the moment he voiced it.

"No," she said. "But I'm sure Ivy knows. She runs extensive background checks on all the operatives. It's her job to ensure the safety of the team. It makes sense she would know about the threats each of us carry."

"Grief isn't a threat, Jocelyn." The irony of that statement wasn't lost on him. Because he'd buried his, too. He'd taken everything he remembered about his sister and replaced it with a dark hole that vacuumed up any unwanted emotion so they couldn't hurt him.

"Isn't it?" She faced him, and Baker suddenly found himself missing that wide smile he caught her with every time they'd come across each other in town. "Losing our loved ones altered our entire beings. There are studies that prove traumatic events such as ours physically change our genes and can be passed down through our prodigy. It lives within us, clawing to get free at any chance our guard is down. It waits for just the right moment to sabotage us, and I can't afford for that to happen in the middle of an assignment."

"So you keep it to yourself. Pretend it doesn't bother you." Just as he'd done all this time. Though it was becoming clearer every day he stayed away from the barn that he and his sister had built with their own hands that Linley deserved better. She deserved to be remembered. The good and the bad. No matter how much it hurt. Because living as an entirely different person obviously hadn't worked out the way either of them had hoped. "What if tonight, we don't pretend anymore?"

"What do you mean?" Her hesitation filtered into the inches between them, thick enough for him to reach out and touch.

"I read Maverick's dog tags." Baker skimmed his thumb along her jaw, picking up the slightest change across her skin through touch alone. It was all he needed for his brain to fill in the gaps. As though she'd become part of him. "I know he was your husband's bomb-sniffing dog up until he died. DHS most likely wanted to retire him after your husband's death, maybe even send him to a shelter, but you brought him back home."

Jocelyn didn't answer for a series of calculated breaths. "When Miles was admitted to the hospital for the last time, it was because he collapsed in the middle of an assignment. The cancer had gotten into his bones, and there was no treatment—nothing—that would reverse the damage. Maverick was the one who got him to safety, then lay by Miles's bed until his final moments." She swallowed hard. "He wouldn't obey the commands of any other operatives. It got to the point Maverick became aggressive if anyone came close to my husband's body. Even handlers he'd worked beside in the field, but most especially the nurses. He hated them."

Her laugh slipped free and settled the anxiety building in his chest. "The hospital wanted Animal Control brought in so they could remove the body without getting bitten, but Mile's superior asked them to hold off as long as possible. Looking back, I think Maverick was waiting. For me."

Her voice warbled, but the dim lighting kept Baker from seeing her tears. "He waited there without food, without water or sleep. Protecting the one person who loved him most in the world, and I will always be grateful for that. It's hard to imagine he has any of those same feelings for me, but after Miles died and we were learning to live without him in our lives, I got so sick. To the point I couldn't get out of bed most mornings. I wasn't eating or sleeping or able to live up to my duties. Maverick was the one who pulled me out of the darkness and gave me the courage to take an opportunity we could both benefit from."

"One that brought you to Socorro," Baker said.

"Yeah." She craned her head to one side, presumably watching the German shepherd sleep in his too-small dog bed set up in one corner of the room. "He helped me get back on my feet. Though we both knew we couldn't go back to the way things were. I'd never be able to leave him behind if I got called up, and he couldn't go back to DHS, even with a handler he knew. We both had to figure out a way to move on. Without Miles. And for all the trouble he gives me, I know he loves me, too."

Baker angled his hands onto her hips and dragged

her close as a feeling of empathy and desire and attachment burst through him. He notched Jocelyn's chin higher with the side of his index finger and pressed his mouth to hers. "Does this mean I'm competing for your affections with a German shepherd? Because I feel now is the time to tell you I'm not really a dog person."

Chapter Eleven

Today she would live in the moment. Unless it was unpleasant. In which case she'd eat a cookie. Jocelyn stretched her toes to the end of the bed, coming face-to-face with the man tucked beneath the sheets beside her.

Sensations she hadn't allowed herself to feel since her husband's death quaked through her as memories of her and Baker's night surfaced. It'd been perfect. He'd been perfect. Respectful, careful and passionate all at once. They'd held each other long past cresting pleasure and fallen asleep secure in the moment.

She'd done it. Taken that first step toward moving on. For the first time since receiving the news Miles had passed, she felt…liberated. The weight of guilt and shame and judgment had lost its hold sometime between when Baker had kissed her and now. She'd almost forgotten how to breathe without it.

Early morning sunlight streaked across the sky, and while she normally liked to lie in bed to take it in, she couldn't tear herself away from the harsh beauty of the man beside her. The bruising around his temple was starting to turn lighter shades of green and yellow. The tension had bled from his expression. No longer the high-strung chief of police, she was getting a full view of the man beneath the mantle. Just Baker.

Jocelyn traced her thumb along his lower lip, eager to feel his mouth on hers once more. But she'd let him sleep. That seemed to be the only place he felt safe after everything he'd survived. His skin warmed under her touch, as it had last night, and she couldn't help but lose herself in this moment. One where they had permission to be still—content, even. Where the world didn't demand or push or threaten. She couldn't remember the last time she'd just let herself…be. Always afraid the bad thoughts and feelings would find her if she slowed down enough to let them in.

It'd taken a while to figure out that keeping her hands busy and her mind engaged distracted her from the heaviness she carried. It'd been a lifeline for so long, she couldn't actually remember what it felt like to live in the moment. But this… This was different. This was easy. Comfortable. Watching Baker sleep somehow hijacked her brain into believing she was safe here. With him. Her chest incrementally released the defensiveness always taking the wheel, and for the first time in years, she let herself relax. Because of him. Because of his willingness to take on her grief, to share it with her, to lighten the load.

And she'd done the same for him. Listened to his stories about his sister, of the two of them growing up back east and all the trouble they'd gotten into being so close in age. Only eleven months apart. About how once their mother had passed, their father had remarried and started his life over with a new family. Forgetting what he'd already had.

Maverick's dog tags rang through the room.

"Oh, no. Maverick, stop!" Jocelyn tossed her covers and hit the floor to intercept the shepherd. Too late. The overly loud ping of Maverick's bell pierced through the silence. And she froze.

"I'm up!" Baker shot upright in the bed. Every delicious muscle rippled through his back and chest as he reached for the weapon stashed beneath his pillow, and he took aim. At her.

Jocelyn raised her hands in surrender, her heart in her throat. "We're not dying. It's just Maverick. He needs to go out."

"Maverick?" Seconds split between heavy breathing and the pound of her pulse at the base of her neck. His gun hand and weapon collapsed into his lap. "For crying out loud."

"Sorry. I tried to beat him to it." She twisted the bedroom door deadbolt and let Maverick into the hall. He'd find his way outside through one of the dog doors before heading to breakfast with the other K-9s. Closing the door behind her dog, she padded to Baker's side of the bed. "I wanted you to be able to sleep a bit longer."

He leaned back against the pillows, and she went with him. "Well, that's out of the question now."

She settled her ear over his chest as the sun brightened the sky on the other side of the window. Pulling the comforter over them, Baker tucked her into his side until they breathed as one. She felt her heart rate settle back into comfortable territory, as though every cell in her body had attuned to every cell in his. Funny what surviving two bombings and fighting for each other's lives did for a relationship.

A relationship.

She hadn't really considered the words until now. Was that what this was? When the investigation ended and they had this new bomber—whoever he was—in custody, would they still have this? Or had last night been a one-time moment of comfort?

Ever since she'd lost Miles, she'd been running from this exact encounter. But now, relearning how to be close to someone, relearning how to trust and love meant it could all be taken away. By illness, by betrayal and the kind of work she did. But her soul craved that connection, and denying it would only make things worse.

Jocelyn committed right then. To make this moment last as long as possible. To not let the past infiltrate the present. No matter how much it hurt to let go. "What happens now, Baker? After all of this is done. What do you see happening between us?"

"Guess I haven't given it much thought," he said. "But I want this to be honest. I like you. More than I thought I could like a mercenary." He took her elbow to his gut with ease, his laugh filling not just the room but the empty places inside of her. The ones she'd denied existed. "Truth is, I'm not sure I could go back to the way things were. You on one side of the divide. Me on the other. We're a team. And I want it to stay that way."

A light that had nothing to do with the sunrise flooded through her. Not forced or created out of a sense of survival. Genuine warmth that could only come from one source. Hope.

"Me, too." But he wanted this to be honest. Something she wasn't sure she could reciprocate. Because the moment she admitted her darkest shame to him, she'd have to face it herself. And she wasn't ready to lose what they had. Not yet.

She ran her fingertips up his forearm, to the measure of warped skin spanning from his elbow to his wrist. She sat up, angling across his lap to get a better look. "What's this?"

"A burn scar." His voice scraped along his throat, barely audible. "Got it the day I found Linley in the barn. Most of the structure was still standing by some miracle, but one of the beams failed when I was inside. I tried to protect myself with my arm. Ended up with this piece of art."

"Marc De Leon had scars like this—burn scars. I remember them from his arrest photo." She memorized the rise and fall of the pattern burned into his arm as pieces of the puzzle they'd taken on flirted at the edge of her mind. Her instincts pushed her out of the bed and had her reaching for her rob draped across the end. She cinched it as carpet caught on the laceration across the bottom of her heel and threatened to slow her down, but this was important.

"Yeah. I catalogued them after the arrest. Scars,

fingerprints and tattoos. It's standard protocol so we can register him with the National Crime Information Center, but what does that have to do with anything?" The bed creaked under his weight as he sat up.

Jocelyn shuffled through the file she'd put together on the cartel lieutenant. ATF believed Marc De Leon had been recruited as an adult and risen up Sangre por Sangre's ranks in large part due to his proclivity for brutality and following orders to the letter. But he'd made a mistake. He'd killed an Alpine Valley woman three months ago. Jane Doe. He'd stepped out of line. But what if it hadn't been a mistake? What if it'd been a pattern?

She pulled a photo of Jane Doe free from the file, noting charred skin, curled limbs and missing teeth. An entire legacy of violence and death. Marc De Leon hadn't just killed the woman. He'd made her unrecognizable. To everyone but who he'd wanted the message sent to. "When was Linley killed?"

"Two years ago." Baker slipped free of the bed and reached for the sweats piled on the floor. "Why?"

"Cartels like the misery they cause. They use fear and grief and pain to keep towns like Alpine Valley in line and unwilling to turn on them. That's why they came after your sister. The soldiers who burned down your barn and murdered Linley knew you weren't there that day. They wanted you to see what they'd done." She spread out the photos taken of the scene where Jane Doe had been recovered. A tire had been strung around the victim's neck—just like Linley's—

but only after a device packed into a Kevlar vest had destroyed her insides. "They wanted you scared and compliant."

Baker stepped into her, his chest pressed against her arm. The contact was enough to keep her grounded but didn't diminish the buzz of anticipation for him to see what she saw in the details. "I'm going to need you to get to your point a lot faster, Jocelyn."

"You thought Linley's and Jane Doe's murders were connected, that they were the work of the same bomber." She handed him the photo of Jane Doe. "With good reason. The Ghost used the same devices, same amount of explosive packed into Kevlar, same brand of tires strung around their necks after the victims were already dead. But I don't think Jane Doe was the intended target. I think the cartel used her to deliver a message."

"Linley was a message for me." He stared down at the photo so hard she thought he might tear through it with his mind. "And Jane Doe was left for Ponderosa's Chief Trevino to back off. Right before they killed him."

THE PATTERN WAS becoming clearer by the minute.

All this time he'd been hunting the Ghost—a bomber who'd killed not only his sister but an innocent woman—and the bastard had been right in front of him.

Tremors worked through his hands as Baker rushed to dress into his uniform. This wasn't how this was supposed to end. He'd wanted to confront the son of a bitch, to show him all the pain and destruction he'd caused. To punish him. But Marc De Leon was dead. "I had him. I should've seen it before now. If I hadn't been so focused on justice for Linley, I could've saved Ponderosa's chief from...this."

"Marc De Leon didn't want you to see it, Baker." Jocelyn moved to reach out to him but seemingly thought better of it halfway. Hell, she was pulling away from him. After everything they'd worked through last night, he had to go and ruin it. "He was good at what he did."

"Why would someone else blow up my station to destroy evidence against Marc De Leon and claim to be the Ghost?" The question left his mouth more forcibly than he'd meant, and Baker caught himself losing his tight control on his anger. Just as he had after Linley's death. It wasn't him. It was the vengeful demon inside of him, and right now, there was a very thin line holding it at bay as his failures came into account. "How does that make sense?"

She didn't answer for a series of breaths, to the point that Baker sensed she might turn around and walk right out that door. Pinpricks stabbed at the back of his neck. He was on the brink of falling off that edge of reason.

"Tell me how I'm supposed to stay in this investigation when I can't even send the man I've wanted to arrest for two years to jail. What kind of chief of police does that make me?" The tremors were coming less frequent the longer he focused on her. On the way her right shoulder rose slightly higher than her left when she inhaled. The fact that the hair framing her face had a soft streak of lighter color. Baker memorized everything he could about her to keep himself from losing his mind, but he wasn't strong enough to keep fighting. Maybe he never had been. "Tell me what to do next."

"We know someone else is using Marc De Leon's recipe for the bombs. Socorro is trying to track down the sales of the nitroglycerin, but it's going to take time. There are still a lot of construction and mining operations that use it by the bulk. It would be easy for a few measures to go missing from one of the sites." She paused for a moment. "And I've reached out to a few contacts in ATF. They'll follow up with any reports of missing ordnance. Though if they haven't heard of any to this point, it's likely the bomber covered his tracks." Jocelyn took a step closer to him, breaking into his personal space. "Which means he's far more dangerous than we estimated. If we can't figure out how much nitroglycerin is missing, then we can't predict the next attack."

A shiver raced along his spine at the thought. The Ghost—at least, the man he'd believed to be the cartel's resident bomber—had gone out of his way to ensure Baker had been present at both bombings. First at the station when the son of a bitch had destroyed the evidence linking Marc De Leon to the death of Jane Doe. Then ambushing them at the lieutenant's compound.

He took a full breath. If Marc De Leon was Sangre por Sangre's Ghost, why would another bomber blow up proof he was guilty of murder and then take De Leon out? Had the cartel wanted to tie up a loose end that might admit to sixteen other incidents connecting back to the cartel? "Has there been any response from Sangre por Sangre for what happened at the compound?"

"Now that you mention it, we haven't seen any movement on their part. Cash would've let us know." Jocelyn grabbed for her cell phone, lighting up the screen. "Kind of hard to miss an explosion that almost buried an entire town. It's all over the news. Surrounding towns are sending in aid and raising funds for the cleanup. Jones has been handling the influx in help so we can focus on finding the bomber, while Cash has been keeping an eye on the cartel. You think they're keeping their distance for a reason?"

"Cartel soldiers are arrested all the time. My deputies and I have put the cuffs on more than our fair share, but the response is always the same. No one talks. Because if you give up the cartel, you won't even make it to your cell." Baker was trying to make sense of the thoughts in his head as fast as he could, but there were still too many moving pieces. The man they'd encountered in the desert had described the pain of watching someone he loved tortured and killed in front of him. Had said Baker had been spared. "No. I'm starting to think this is about something else altogether."

"Like what?" she asked.

"Whoever set that device in the station placed it in the evidence room. I think we were right in figuring it was purposefully detonated to destroy evidence in Marc De Leon's murder case." Baker paced across the room, to the window and back. "But how could the bomber have known we'd go to De Leon's compound? How was he waiting for us unless he knew we'd be there?"

"Easy to draw that conclusion once we realized the first bomb had been a means to destroy evidence in the murder investigation." Jocelyn leaned back against the desk built into the main wall of her room. No family photos staring back from shelves. No personal touches added over the course of her tenure with Socorro. This wasn't a home for her and Maverick. It was just a temporary way station until something else came along. "Could be the bomber has studied your protocols, knew you'd want to take up a case this big yourself rather than assigning it to one of your deputies. Especially if he knows what happened in your past. He went out there to set things up and then waited for us."

Damn, he'd missed this. Someone to bounce ideas off of, to solve puzzles with and test his limits. The feeling of partnership. Like he'd had with Linley. Building and working for something greater than the both of them. Sure, his deputies had his back in any given situation. They were there to do their job, and they did it well, but that didn't make them friends. More like acquaintances who sometimes took turns to bring in doughnuts.

But Jocelyn… She was different. She was more than an acquaintance. More than a friend. She was everything he'd needed over these past couple days—and everything he wanted for his life. Who else was capable of looking him right in the eye and telling him he'd been chasing a ghost? Who else surprised him on more occasion than he could count? She was the kind of woman who genuinely put others' needs before her own, just to give them a sense of peace, and hell, if that wasn't one of the most beautiful things he'd ever witnessed. Not to mention the explosive pleasure she'd ignited in him last night. Jocelyn Carville had ambushed him when he'd least expected it, and he never wanted to give her up.

Baker slowed his pacing. "Or the bomber wasn't there for me at all."

"What do you mean? He strapped a device into your Kevlar and handcuffed you to your steering wheel. The only reason you're still standing here is because you figured out how to disrupt the pager's receiver used to trigger the bomb." Confusion was etched above her eyebrows, and with good reason. "He was going to kill you, Baker. He tried to kill both of us, or have you forgotten there was a bullet in my shoulder less than twenty-four hours ago?"

"Because I was in his way." It was the only thing that made sense. "That's why he shot you. We were nothing but obstacles to what he really wanted."

"The Ghost." Her bottom lip pulled away from the top. "Marc De Leon."

"Everything that's happened since that first explosion at the station has been centered around him." A flash of nervous excitement spiraled through him until Baker couldn't stop the words from forming. This was it. This was how they found the son of a bitch. "Sangre por Sangre soldiers are protected on the inside. Alpine Valley PD had evidence Marc De Leon murdered that woman during the raid, but what if a handful of years in prison wasn't enough for our bomber? What if he wanted the Ghost to suffer a hell of a lot more, without protection and with no chance of some defense attorney giving him an easy way out?"

Because Baker had wanted the exact same thing. For the man who'd murdered his sister and burned his world to the ground to suffer. That drive for revenge had been in his head from the moment he woke every morning and was the very last thought on his mind as he ended the day. Everything he'd done had been to make the bastard feel what Baker had felt upon finding Linley in that barn.

Jocelyn shoved away from the desk with her uninjured hand. "He wanted to add you as a notch in the Ghost's belt to double down on the charges. But why destroy evidence in the murder investigation? Why take away a sure conviction and a chance for Jane Doe to get the justice she deserves?"

The truth hit harder than he was ready for.

"Because the death of a second chief of police by the cartel would bring in the big guns." His blood ran cold at the mere suggestion. "One woman killed by one of their soldiers doesn't get much attention except from the people in Alpine Valley. By now, everyone has forgotten about her and moved on with their lives, but if two officers are murdered at the hands of the cartel?"

Jocelyn's expression fell, and damn it, he couldn't deny how much he hated seeing her without a smile. Forced or otherwise. "The feds would have no other choice than to call in every agency on their payroll, including Socorro."

"We've been thinking this is has been a targeted effort. One man trying to kill another, but we were wrong." Baker scrubbed a hand down his face. "The bomber wants to start a war."

Chapter Twelve

She couldn't be a smart cookie with a crumbly attitude.

Jocelyn hauled herself from the passenger seat of the loaner SUV she'd borrowed from Jones. With her vehicle in a million pieces and her shoulder in a sling, she'd have to rely on the rest of team to get her around for a while. Not a comfortable feeling, but she had too many other things on her mind.

Finding a bomber before he launched a war with the Sangre por Sangre cartel, for one.

She let Maverick out of the back seat as she surveyed the scene.

The landslide had been worse than she'd thought. Rain pelted against her face and soaked into the ground. It made balance harder for the volunteer cleanup crew trying not to slide down the new hill and threatened to land her on her ass. Mud, rock, cement chunks and wood framing had flooded through an entire street of homes. Far too many homes had been lost, and now there was nothing left but their roofs peeking out from areas Fire and Rescue had dug out.

This was a disaster in every sense of the word.

It would take months to excavate, and what happened to those families in the meantime? Jones had reported they'd been evacuated before the slide, but where were they supposed to go now?

"You okay?" Baker rounded the hood of the SUV, setting his hand beneath her slung elbow as support.

"My arm is just a bit sore." An understatement of the highest degree. The wound in her shoulder wasn't just sore. It was on fire. The last of the pain medication she'd received in the medical suite had burned off—most likely with help of last night's heart-racing activities—leaving her in a world of pain she hadn't known physically existed. "I'll be fine."

"You sure? Because you look like you're about to fall over." No hint of humor in his voice, which meant she looked as good as she felt. "Why don't you wait in the car? I can check in with the bomb squad alone."

"I said I'll be fine." Frustration had seeped past her control, and an instant shot of shame and embarrassment knifed through her as Baker removed his hand from her elbow. Jocelyn forced that practiced smile back in place. Everything was fine as long as she was smiling. She could do this. Because waiting in the car while the rest of her team and Baker worked this case wasn't an option.

She navigated up a sharp incline to where the rest of the volunteers and the bomb squad had set up a command center under a canvas pavilion. "Let's just see what they've found."

"Sure." He followed on her heels. Not as close as she'd come to expect. He was keeping his distance, and her skin heated despite the drop in temperature down here in the canyon and shade.

She watched her step as she climbed, but every movement took something out of her she couldn't really afford to give up. Agony was tearing at the edges of the bullet wound. Not to mention the stab wound beneath her Kevlar, but she wouldn't let it get to her. She just had to get through to the other side.

Maverick pressed into her leg as though she was about to collapse. Seemed Baker wasn't the only one doubting her capabilities today.

Jones offered her a hand as she summited the last few feet to man-made flat ground and dragged her upward. "Wasn't expecting you to make it out here today. You good?"

"Fine. How's it going here?" she asked.

"The excavators you recruited from Deer Creek and Ponderosa should be here this afternoon." The combat controller pointed out over the ridge that hadn't been put there naturally. "Right now, the bomb squad is digging to recover any other pieces of the device."

Jocelyn angled her head back to take in the view above. She shaded her face against the onslaught of rain pecking at them. A massive chuck of rock had broken away from the canyon wall, leaving the outline of an oversized bite. Her foot sank deeper into the shifting earth. "How long are they estimating the cleanup will take?"

"A couple months at least," Jones said. "The rains make it more difficult, but we're moving as fast as we can. The Bureau of Land Management sent in a geologist. From what he can tell, the threat of more rock coming down on us has passed, but we've been instructed to keep on alert. Just in case."

Shouts echoed off the canyon wall that'd always stood as a protection to this town, and the pain inside of her intensified. Jocelyn clamped a hand on her shoulder.

Jones's gaze cut to Baker, then back to her.

"Joce, maybe you should take a break." Baker stepped into her line of vision. "The pain meds Dr. Piel gave you are in my pack in the car. I'll get you one."

"No." The muscles in her jaw ached under the pressure of her back teeth. She bit back a moan and squeezed her eyes tight, waiting for the pain to pass. It didn't, and she couldn't stop the tears from pricking at her eyes. One deep breath. Two. The burn receded slightly, and Jocelyn dared to remove the pressure of her hand. Straightening, she faced both men. "I don't…need it."

Maverick *gruffed* beside her. He'd always been able to tell when she was lying.

"All right, then. Captain Pennymeyer is waiting for us in the command tent." Jones took the lead, cutting across the makeshift camp.

The sound of shovels, wheelbarrows and heavy breathing cut through the patter of rain as residents, Fire and Rescue and two deputies Jocelyn recognized as Alpine Valley PD worked to dig out the affected houses.

The combat controller held the flap of the pavilion

open for them, revealing a grouping of cops inside. The Albuquerque bomb squad. The man hunched over the laptop in the center straightened at their approach. His once muscular frame had gone soft. Too large on top, not enough stability in his lower half. The effect said while the officer in charge ran his department well, he wasn't usually out in the field.

"Chief Halsey. I'm Captain Pennymeyer." The bomb squad's commanding officer extended his hand past Jocelyn to meet Baker's. "We've managed to uncover several materials used in the device detonated at your station to compare with those recovered here."

"Grateful to have you." Baker shook before withdrawing. There was an invisible bond between cops and military units. She'd had that once, on tour, but having a captain of the bomb squad blatantly disregard her presence only added to the pulse in her shoulder. "This is Jocelyn Carville from Socorro Security. She saw the device before it detonated inside the compound."

"Then by all means, Ms. Carville, tell me if we got this right." Pennymeyer maneuvered around the standing desk he'd created toward a long table covered in plastic. Pieces of wire, motherboard and mud-coated plastic had been separated and studiously labeled for study. "Your statement said you saw the device tucked up into the rafters of the home. That right?"

Her mouth dried as she took in all the fractured pieces that'd once made a whole. The intricacy and placement of every one of these materials had nearly destroyed an entire town. "Yes."

"Did you see anything specific?" the captain asked. "Were there any wires leading away from the device? A countdown clock, or maybe you caught the branding on the battery before it went off?"

Her mind went blank as pain clawed down her arm and into her chest. She clung to her sling with her free hand as the world tipped slightly. Scouring the table, she tried to make all these tiny pieces fit into a puzzle her brain was desperate to put together. Had she seen the branding on the battery? Heat flared into her face and neck. "I don't... I don't know. I only got a glimpse of it before I ran for the patio door."

The captain stepped off to one side, and it was only then that she realized a blueprint of Marc De Leon's compound had been tacked to the flexible wall above the table. "Your statement reports you saw the device tucked into the rafters of the kitchen. Is that correct?"

Her heart rate rocketed into overdrive. She'd already been through all of this. The last reserves of her control bled dry. "If you've read my statement, why are you asking me again?"

Silence enveloped the tent, all eyes on her.

She tried to breathe through the pain, but it wasn't working this time. It crescendoed until it was all she felt. Consuming her inch by inch.

Captain Pennymeyer directed his attention downward to his table of explosive goodies. "We're just trying to get the most accurate information, Ms. Carville. It's been known that victims caught in an event like this tend to remember more a couple days after they've had time to recover."

"I'm not a victim." A barb of annoyance poked at her insides.

"Of course. I didn't mean…" The captain's face flushed, and his oversized upper body seemed to deflate right in front of her. "I apologize. I didn't mean any insult. I understand you've been through something quite traumatic."

Baker inched closer. "Will you give us a minute, Captain?" He lowered his voice. "Let's get some air."

She wanted to argue, but being inside the too-small tent packed with cops was getting to her. Cold air worked into her lungs once outside, but she couldn't distract her body from focusing on the throbbing in her shoulder.

Baker set his hand against her lower back, guiding her roughly ten feet from the men waiting for her confirmation that they'd recovered every piece of the bomb that'd brought down the compound on top of Alpine Valley. He pulled out a bright orange, cylindrical container with a white top from his front pocket. "Here. I had Jones grab your pain meds from the car."

Twisting off the cap with his palm, he dragged one of the pills inside free and offered it to her.

Every nerve in her body went on the defense. She took a physical step back. "I told you I didn't want it."

"You'd rather be in debilitating pain while we're here?" He countered her escape, keeping his voice low enough so as not to be overheard by anyone else. "Not sure you noticed, but if you weren't talking to me right now, I'd think you were dead you're so pale. You're having trouble focusing, and you just bit off the head of the guy running this investigation."

She couldn't take her attention off the pill in his hand.

"Joce, everyone in that tent knows you were shot," he said. "None of them are going to think any less of you for taking the edge off."

She shook her head. She could hardly breathe. "I can't."

"What is this? Some kind of punishment for what happened?" Confusion and a heavy dose of frustration had Baker dropping the pain med back into the container. He screwed the top on. "For not being there when your husband died? Is that it? You've convinced yourself you deserve to suffer? You were shot and stabbed by a piece of debris, for crying out loud. I'd say that's enough penance to last a lifetime."

The pain burned through her, and no amount of distraction was taking it away. Jocelyn headed across the cleanup site, the sound of Maverick's dog tags in her ears. Her shepherd knew she was on the brink of going over the edge. "No. It's not like that."

"Then what is it like?" Baker followed. "Tell me."

She turned on him. There was no hiding it. Not anymore. "I'm a recovering addict."

An addict.

Baker didn't know what to say to that, what to *think*.

He tightened his grip on the medication bottle, his hand slick with sweat. "I don't..." Clearing his throat, he tried to get his head back into the game. "I don't understand. You were on morphine in the medical unit after what happened up there. You didn't say anything."

Jocelyn released her hold on her shoulder, trying to make it look as though nothing got to her. She had a habit of doing that. Pretending. "Dr. Piel doesn't know my medical history. The nurses at the clinic that first time we were caught in the bombing at the police station had my chart. They knew not to put me on anything stronger than ibuprofen."

"You're going to have to start from the beginning." Baker found himself backing up, adding more than a couple of feet between them. "Because what you're saying right now doesn't make sense."

"What more is there to explain?" Her expression fell into something that could only be categorized as hollowness. As though she'd told this story so many times, she'd disassociated from the emotional toll it took. Though from what she'd just said, not everybody knew. "I lost my husband, Baker. I blamed myself for not being there in his final moments. I was getting messages from his friends, his family, calls from his doctor—all asking me why I wasn't there. Because all he'd wanted in his final moments was for me to be by his side, and I let him down."

Baker tried to swallow past the swelling in his throat, but there was no point. "So when you said you got sick after his death, you meant…"

"The pain hurt so much. I tried everything I could think of to make it stop, but nothing worked. The grief was crushing me, and I didn't know what else to do." The heartache was still pressing in on her. He could see it in her eyes, in the way she practically crumpled in on herself. "One night it got so bad, I thought I might hurt myself, but I found Miles's old pain meds in the bathroom cabinet. I took one." Her voice evened out. "All it took was one."

"You started taking the pills more often." Baker studied the orange pill bottle in his hand right there in the middle of what was left of his town. He'd responded to overdoses of all kinds while working this job. Mothers who'd only wanted to be able to do it all with a touch of ecstasy. Teens who started sniffing coke in the back seat of the bus on the way to school to fit in with their peers. A middle schooler who'd binged two bottles of cough medicine to get drunk. Sangre por Sangre had made it all possible— easier—to drag an ordinary life through the mud. And it turned out, he'd been partnered with an addict all this time. Bringing his gaze back to hers, he pocketed the pills, just in case the sight of them was enough to trigger something compulsive in her. "How did you stop?"

"I didn't. At least not before it got worse." Sweat slipped from her hairline. One push. That was all it'd take, and she'd collapse from the pain. How the hell was she still standing there as though she could take on the world? "The pills ran out. I went to my doctor. He wouldn't help me. Neither would any of the others. The military discharged me under honorable conditions, but I couldn't face the truth—that I was alone. So I did what I thought I had to at the time."

His heart threatened to beat straight out of his chest. Baker licked at dry lips, but it didn't do a damn bit of good. Because he knew what was coming next. "You found something stronger to replace the pills."

"I convinced myself I could handle it." She dropped her chin to her chest, shutting him out. "It was supposed to be a temporary fix, but the longer I used, the more I realized I didn't want to stop. I didn't want to hurt every time I walked through the door or thought about my husband. I don't really remember a whole lot during that time, but it got bad enough no one—not even my friends, my unit or my family—could help."

Jocelyn seemed to let go of something heavy, as though the rain were washing away the weight she'd carried. She stepped toward him. "But I'm in recovery now. I got myself into NA. I have a sponsor I check in with. I've been clean for over a year. It's… hard. Especially when I'm injured in the field, but I don't want to go back to being numb, Baker. I don't. And with you, I finally feel like I can leave that part of me behind. That there's more to my life than my mistakes."

A thousand questions rushed to the surface, but all he focused on was the hollowness in his chest. There were a limited number of organizations where she could've gotten drugs like the ones she'd talked about, and the entire town of Alpine Valley had slowly been dying because of one of them. "Where did you get the drugs?"

That shadow of enthusiasm and hope—nothing like when he'd first met her—drained from her expression. "Why does that matter?"

"I think you know why it matters, Jocelyn," he said.

Understanding cemented her expression in place. "Seems like you already know the answer you're looking for."

"From a cartel." He couldn't believe this. All this time, he'd trusted her to be on his side of the fight, but she'd kept a major part of her life out of the equation. Lied to him. "I can't tell you how many times I've walked into one of these houses and found a kid barely breathing because of the crap he put in his arm or describe how many babies will have serious complications throughout their lives because their mothers won't look at the people they really are in the mirror. And now you're telling me you're one of them."

Her face ticked at one side, as though he thrown a physical punch. "It's…it's not the same. You know it's not. I changed. I got help so I could start my life over —"

"Has it worked?" he asked. "You paste on that smile and try to find an upside to everything so you don't have to feel your loss. You're so desperate to avoid reality, you've created your own. Christmas parties, cookie bake-offs, movie nights and forced team dinners. You might not be on the drugs anymore, but you're still looking for ways to numb yourself, Jocelyn."

He regretted the words the moment they left his

mouth, but Baker couldn't seem to pull back. The cartel had taken everything he'd ever cared about. The bed and breakfast he built with his own hands, his sister. And now Jocelyn.

"Is that why you started working for Socorro? The reason you came to Alpine Valley?" Baker couldn't stop the words. "To make yourself feel like you were actually fighting the cartel? So you could pretend to be the hero? You outright supported the very people you've been investigating with me. You see that, don't you? You made them stronger while everyone in this town is simply trying to survive."

Tears glittered in her eyes. "And what have you been doing since the cartel killed your sister, Baker? Because I can tell you what you haven't been doing. You haven't been confronting your pain. You might not be going about it the same way I did, but you're just as guilty as I am of trying to escape."

"You might be right," he said. "But I wasn't the one who kept that from my partner."

She didn't have an answer for him.

In truth, he didn't want one. He didn't want any excuses. He didn't want to see reason. Baker pointed an index finger at her. "You know, I thought you were different. I thought we really had something, that it would be worth it to make it work between us, but I can't spend the rest of my life wondering if you're going to relapse or if I'm going to find you dead from an overdose."

He unpocketed the pills and threw them at her feet. The container lid burst free, sprinkling her meds in a two-foot radius. It was childish and petty and didn't do a damn thing to release the tightness in his chest. "Do whatever you want with these. Consider our partnership terminated. I'm done."

"That's it?" Her voice wavered from behind. "After everything we've survived together, after everything we've shared, you're going to condemn me and what we have because of a mistake? I thought you of all people would understand."

He didn't. He didn't understand how someone he'd convinced himself would never betray her beliefs could undermine his trust so quickly. "You were wrong."

Jones Driscoll and Captain Pennymeyer stood at the door flap of the command center, unmoving. Seemed the entire site had turned its attention to him. Waiting for his answer. But he didn't owe them anything. And he didn't owe Jocelyn, either.

Baker kept on walking back toward the command tent. Part of him knew while he hadn't taken up numbing himself the way she had, he'd taken this job to get back at the bastards that'd destroyed his life. He'd lived off of revenge, but he hadn't given up his morals in the process.

"Fine." A low whistle cut through the site, and Maverick's dog tags clashing together reached Baker's senses over the soft tick of rain. "But the next time you're facing down a bomb, don't call me for help."

A car door slammed a moment before the SUV's engine caught.

He crossed back into the command tent, knowing all too well the officers and operatives inside had heard every word. Baker took up position in front of the table with the deconstructed pieces of the bomb that should've killed him—would have if it hadn't been for Jocelyn. His heart dropped in his chest as he caught the tail end of her vehicle through the open tent flap.

"Show's over. We have a bomber to find."

Chapter Thirteen

She would've given up her last cookie for him.

Tears clouded her vision as Jocelyn floored the accelerator. She'd never been so humiliated in her life. Not just by her darkest shame but by having it exposed in the middle of a crime scene, surrounded by her team and other officers she worked with. But that wasn't what hurt the most. A hook cut through her stomach as Baker's words echoed on repeat.

I can't spend the rest of my life wondering if you're going to relapse or if I'm going to find you dead from an overdose.

His concerns were valid. Every day she fought the same demons. Every day she went to bed knowing she'd done her best and tallied another day of survival. Because that was what she was doing. *Surviving.* Constantly on the defense of a threat. But she'd never expected it to come from Baker.

The pain in her shoulder was nothing compared to the agony closing in around her heart. Jocelyn swiped at her face as a pair of headlights inched into the rearview mirror. She'd escaped the town limits, halfway between Alpine Valley and Socorro. Not nearly enough distance to put between her and what'd just happened. Open desert expanded ahead. Ten minutes back to headquarters. Then she could pack and get the hell away from this place.

Maverick whined from the back cargo area. His face centered in the mirror. As much as he preferred to cuddle with a stick rather than her, he picked up on her emotions better than most humans. He was hurting, too.

"I know, but we can't go back." She tightened her grip on the steering wheel. While she hadn't envisioned anything past this investigation, she'd gotten attached to this place. To Baker. He'd unlocked something in her over the past few days. Hope. Trust. Joy. He'd taken her pain and internalized it for himself, leaving her lighter and freer than she'd felt in a long time. He'd listened to her. Convinced her that grief didn't always have to call the shots. That she could be more than an addict. And she loved him for gifting her that relief. Damn it, she loved him.

But he'd made his opinion on her history clear. His personal agenda against the cartel ensured there was nothing she could do or say to change his mind. "There's nothing left for us here."

The headlights behind her got closer. Recognition filled in the paint job along the sides of the vehicle. Alpine Valley PD. Every instinct she owned asked her to slow down and pull over, that she should at least give Baker the chance to apologize, but she'd made her point clear, too. The crossbar lights lit up with red-and-blue strobes. The piercing chirp of the siren triggered her nerves. She tried to make out the face in the driver's seat through the rearview mirror. "Keep trying, but I'm not pulling over."

Jocelyn focused on the road ahead. A couple more miles. As much as she hated the idea of hiding out at Socorro, it was the one place he couldn't get to her.

The growl of an engine penetrated through the cabin of the SUV a split second before the patrol car tapped her bumper. The jolt ricocheted through the entire vehicle and caused her front tires to skid slightly.

Warning lightninged through her. She hiked herself higher in the driver's seat to get a better view. She didn't pull over, so now he was going to run her off the road? She was going fifty miles an hour. "Are you out of your mind? What the hell are you doing?"

The rear vehicle surged again. The hood aimed for one corner of her SUV. And made contact. The back tires of the SUV fishtailed off to one side. Jocelyn jerked in her seat as she lost control of the steering wheel. Maverick's howl registered a split second before the tires caught on something off the side of the road.

Momentum flipped the SUV.

Her stomach shot into her throat as gravity took hold. The seat belt cut into her injured shoulder just before the crash slammed her head forward. Dirt, glass and metal protested, cutting off Maverick's pain-filled cry.

The SUV rolled again. Then settled upside down.

"Maverick." His name mixed with blood in her mouth. He didn't answer. Jocelyn pressed one hand into the ceiling of the vehicle. Glass cut into her palm, and the seat belt had her pinned. The rearview mirror was gone. She couldn't see him in the cargo area. Visceral helplessness cascaded through her as she clawed for the release. No. No. Maverick wasn't dead. Flashes of that phone call, of the moment when she'd learned she hadn't been there for Miles before his death, were superimposed onto the present. All her husband had wanted in his last moments had been to be with her. And she hadn't been there. But she would be there for Maverick. She couldn't lose him. She couldn't lose the last piece of her husband. "I'm coming, baby."

Her shoulder screamed against the pressure of the seat belt. She jabbed her thumb into the release.

Jocelyn hit the roof of the SUV harder than she expected. The bullet wound took the brunt of her weight as she tried to dig her legs out from under the steering wheel. Pure agony rippled pins and needles down into her hand. If she hadn't lost function of her arm before, she had now. Swallowing the scream working up her throat, Jocelyn rolled onto her back. "Come on, Mav."

A car door slammed, distorting the hard pound of her heart at the back of her head. Followed by footsteps.

Not Baker.

Alpine Valley's chief of police would never put someone's life in danger. Jocelyn reached for her sidearm but came up empty. The impact must've ripped it free of her holster. She reached overhead and patted her hand over the bottom of the driver's seat. It wasn't there. Her training kicked in. Tucking her arm into her chest, she wormed her way between the front two seats. She had an entire arsenal at her disposal in the back with Maverick. She just had to—

The back passenger side door ripped open. Sunlight blinded her a split second before rough hands wrapped around her ankles and pulled her from the SUV.

Her attacker threw her from the vehicle.

Head snapping back, Jocelyn tried to roll with the force. She landed face down, her arm pinned beneath her. Trying to suck in a full breath, she caught sight of a shadow casting above her.

"And here I thought you'd be happy to see me." The voice played at the edges of her mind—the same voice she'd heard right before she'd taken a bullet in Marc De Leon's compound. "I understand. I mean, it's not like we're friends, but I am doing you and that chief of yours a favor."

She blinked against the spider webs clinging to the sides of her vision. Dirt worked into her mouth, down her throat with every inhale, but all she had attention for was the SUV. And the pool of gasoline leaking down the side. Jocelyn stretched one hand out to pull herself forward. One spark. That was all it would take for her to lose everything. "Maverick."

A heavy boot crushed her fingers into the dry

earth. "Come on now, Carville. You and I both know this has been a long time coming."

The pool of gasoline was growing bigger beneath the vehicle, and there was no sign of Maverick. She had to go. Now. Jocelyn jerked her body to one side, dislodging his pin on her hand. She grabbed for a rock protruding out of the ground and swung at his shin as hard as she could.

The impact knocked the son of a bitch off his feet. She ran for the SUV.

A bullet ripped past her ear and lodged into the hood of the vehicle ahead. Then another. The third shot missed her by mere centimeters as she skidded behind the hood. Pressing her back to the front tires, she tried to get her bearings.

"You have nowhere to go, Carville, and you're wasting my time." His footsteps registered again. This time slower. More careful. As though he was trying to hide his approach.

Jocelyn inched to the back of the vehicle, trying to get a line on the bastard's location through the bulletproof windows. Unfortunately, the coating only made things worse. She couldn't see through them from the outside. Her body demanded rest as she pulled as the back driver's side door.

"There you are." A gun barrel cut into her scalp from behind. "On your feet. Slow. You reach for anything, and the next bullet goes in your head."

How had he moved without her noticing? Jocelyn raised her hands in surrender. She cut her attention to the Alpine Valley patrol vehicle parked twenty feet away. A police officer? "Who are you?"

"Let's just say your chief isn't the only one who wants the cartel to pay for what they've done," he said. "What better way than to frame Sangre por Sangre for your murder?"

"Chief Halsey is smarter than that." Movement registered from the inside the SUV, and her heart shot into her throat. Maverick.

"He may be, but what do you think will happen once Socorro discovers you're dead?" the bomber asked. "Do you think your team will listen to him, or will they pull in every available resource at the government's disposal to put Sangre por Sangre down for good?"

Doubt crept through her.

"That's what this has been all about? Dismantling the cartel?" Baker had been right. This entire investigation had been a cloaked frame job from the beginning. Jocelyn followed the motion of the attacker's weapon, taking that initial step toward the patrol vehicle. All this time, they'd been working for the same end goal. "That's what Alpine Valley PD and Socorro have been trying to accomplish. We're on the same side."

"Yet the cartel somehow still operates without consequences. They raid and kill and take what they want without answering for what they've done." A hardness that sent a chill down her spine added pressure to the gun at her skull. "But with you, I can do what nobody else has been able to."

A low growl pierced her ears. Maverick lunged from the vehicle, fangs bared. He went straight for the bomber's gun hand and ripped the bastard's forearm down.

The attacker's scream was lost to the desert as he tried to regain control of the weapon.

Jocelyn spun. Her fist connected with tissue and bone.

A solid kick landed against Maverick's ribs, and the shepherd backed off with a whine so heart-wrenching it brought up the memory of walking into Miles's hospital room to find Maverick waiting for her.

Air was suctioned out of her chest. She cocked her elbow back for a second strike.

But the bomber was faster. He wrapped his hand around hers and twisted down. Then slammed his forehead into her face.

She hit the ground.

BAKER COULDN'T FORCE himself to focus on the puzzle pieces in front of him. No matter how long he'd stared at them, he couldn't find anything to identify their bomber. The son of a bitch had covered his tracks too well. But worse, he couldn't stop thinking about Jocelyn. About what he'd said to her in those final moments.

"Take a break, Halsey." Jones slammed a hand into Baker's back, and the movement nearly catapulted him forward. "You're going to give yourself an aneurysm. I'll go through everything again. In the meantime, why don't you grab something to eat and catch some sleep. You've been running on fumes for days."

"I'm fine." Baker pinched the bridge of his nose. Truth was, he wasn't fine. He hadn't been for a long time, but having Jocelyn around had helped. Her enthusiasm had been annoying as hell in the beginning. Now he found himself missing it. Her sarcasm had broken through that need to push everyone away. She'd brought out a playful side to him he'd convinced himself had died that day with his sister and given him a sense of adventure. They hadn't just been two people working a case together. They'd been partners. In and out of the field.

And now… Now he felt like he was floating in a thousand different directions without an anchor. Shit. He'd had no right to throw her past in her face like that. She'd lost her husband, the one person she'd counted on being there for her for years. She'd done what she could to survive. Just as he had by making the cartel his personal mission. Two different paths leading to the same place.

He owed her an apology. Hell, he owed her a dozen apologies a day over the next ten years for the way he'd acted. Because despite what he'd said and how he felt about the sickness clawing through Alpine Valley at the cartel's influence, Baker had fallen in love with a mercenary.

"Yeah. You look fine to me." Jones unpocketed a set of keys and tossed them to Baker. "Take my truck. It has a Socorro Security garage pass in the center console. But if anyone asks, you stole it off me. I got you covered."

"Thanks." He let the keys needle into his palm as

he headed for the tent's flap but slowed his escape. "What Jocelyn said earlier about her addiction... I don't want this to come back on her—"

"I already knew." Jones turned back to the blueprints, hands leveraged at his hips. A thick scar ran the length of the combat operator's skull and down beneath his T-shirt. "That's the thing about being part of and living with a team as highly trained as ours twenty-four-seven. You tend to pick up on things. There's nothing we can hide from each other. No matter how hard we try." He released a breath. "That's why I know she's been a lot happier since you started coming around. Her hands aren't permanently stuck in a bowl of dough. She's smiling more. Nothing seems forced like it usually does. I just figured she'd tell us when she was ready. Seems she trusts you, though."

"She did." Baker fisted his hands around the keys.

"She still does. You just have to give her a reason." Jones notched his chin higher, accentuating years of disciplined muscle along his neck and shoulders. "But, Chief, if I hear you throw her past in her face like that again, it won't just be some petty bomber coming for you. Understand? You attack one of us, you attack all of us."

Baker didn't have the voice to answer. He nodded instead and slipped out of the tent. Every nerve ending focused on putting one foot in front of the other. The case, the bomber, the impending war with the cartel—none of it mattered right then. There was only Jocelyn.

"Chief!" Heavy breathing preceded his second-in-command hiking up the slight incline to the plateau of mud, rock and cement. The deputy hiked a thumb over his shoulder. "We just got word of a car fire outside town limits. You can see the smoke from here."

Car fire? Dread pooled at the base of his spine as he caught sight of a thick plume of black smoke directly west. "How long ago?"

"No more than five minutes," the deputy said.

"Anyone injured?" Baker jogged down the slope and hit the unlock button on Jones's keys. Headlights flashed from an oversized black pickup at the end of the street. Ready in case of escape.

"West went to check it out, but his patrol car is missing." The deputy tried to keep up with him.

Disbelief surged high. "He lost his patrol car?"

"No, sir. We believe it was stolen." A hint of embarrassment pecked at the man's neck and face.

Baker's instincts honed in on that cloud of smoke. The base looked as though it was coming from the road cutting between Alpine Valley and Socorro. Which meant... His gut wrenched hard. "Jocelyn."

His entire being shot into battle-ready defense. He raced for Jones's truck. "Get West and round up the Socorro operatives to meet me out there! Now!"

He didn't wait for confirmation. Hauling himself behind the steering wheel, he hit the Engine Start button and threw the truck into gear. Frightened and shocked residents gathered together in groups of two and three as more and more noticed the desert fire. He raced through town as fast as he dared, but the need to get to her as fast as possible had him hugging the accelerator. "I'm coming, Joce. I'm coming."

Trees thinned, exposing the mile-high cliffs on either side of town. Once considered protection, Baker could only look at them now as a threat considering one of them had come crashing down and buried part of his town. But Alpine Valley was resilient. It had to be to survive this long. And though he'd taken up the mantle to protect the people here, he wasn't alone. "Just hang on."

The truck's back tires fishtailed as asphalt gave way to dirt at the border of town. He glanced in the direction of his property, taking in the jagged structure left behind by the bomb and resulting fire, but dragged his attention back to the road. The bed and breakfast, his sister's death, revenge—none of it was strong enough to distract him now. They were in the past. Long gone, and as much as he wanted to hold on to the pain—to get justice for Linley—he had a future to fight for.

Dirt kicked up alongside the truck and pinged off the doors as he picked up speed. The smoke plume had dispersed, and he got his first real look at the fire.

An SUV.

"No. No, no, no." Slamming on the brakes, Baker pulled the truck off the side of the road and threw it into Park. He climbed out of the vehicle, instantly assaulted by the caustic taste and smell of rubber and gasoline. He stuffed his nose and mouth beneath his uniform collar and shaded his eyes before trying to approach, but the heat was too intense. "Jocelyn!"

There wasn't any answer. And he hadn't expected any. If she'd been inside…

Baker lost feeling in his fingers then both arms and that sucking sensation in his chest intensified as the past threatened to pull him in.

The fire grew taller, consuming everything in its path. The entire roof of the barn was missing. Smoke lodged in his throat. He had to get in there. He had to see for himself. The barn door nearly tore off its hinges as the barest touch. He couldn't see, couldn't breathe. Hay burned beneath his shoes, leaving nothing but ash. The horses. Where were the horses?

A sick smell accosted him as he stumbled toward the stall to the right. His stomach emptied right then and there, unable to take the smell. Baker forced himself away from the paddock into the center of the barn.

And he saw her.

Seated against the barn's support beam. Her hands wedged behind her back. Tied. Baker lost his footing. He face-planted mere feet from her bare feet. The dirt crusted in her toenails said she'd been dragged out here. Most likely from the house. Tears and rage and helplessness had him clawing to touch her to make sure she was real. He reached out—

Course fur warmed in his hand.

Baker blinked against the onslaught of sun beating down on him. The fire's heat beaded sweat along his forehead and neck. Cracked earth bit into his knees as he tried to orient himself in the present. He focused on the K-9 leaning into his hand.

"Maverick." Something like relief flooded through

him. Baker scratched behind the shepherd's ears before he pulled the dog closer. "Where is she, buddy?"

A low whine grazed Baker's senses just as he felt
a matted section of fur. Wet and warm. Blood.

"Oh, hell. You fought for her, didn't you? You
tried to help." He hugged Maverick closer, as though
he could somehow reach Jocelyn. "You did good,
boy."

Baker shoved to his feet, fully lodged in the present
thanks to Maverick, and hauled the shepherd into his
chest. "Don't worry. I've got you. I'm going to get you
help. All right? Come on. Let's get you in the truck."

He lifted Maverick into his arms, but a fierce bark
racketed Baker's pulse into dangerous territory. The
German shepherd tried to wiggle free, his claws digging into Baker's skin. Maverick released another
protest—stronger—and Baker set him down. The
K-9 ran around the SUV engulfed in flames.

"Maverick, wait!" Baker pumped his legs as hard
as his muscles allowed. If something happened to
that dog, Jones's warning would mean nothing compared to that of Maverick's handler. He cleared the
car fire as the chirp of a patrol vehicle echoed from
behind. Backup had arrived from Alpine Valley.

But then who did the vehicles cutting across the
horizon belong to?

Baker reached out for Maverick, and the dog took a
seat. Dust and heat blocked a clear view, but he made
out at least a dozen armored, black vehicles a mile out.

Headed for Alpine Valley.

His heart threatened to beat straight out of his chest.

Sangre por Sangre.

"Halsey, what the hell is going on?" Heavy boot-steps pierced through the adrenaline haze. Jones's voice did nothing to ease the panic settling in. "What do you have?"

Air crushed from his chest. "I think we've got a war on our hands."

Chapter Fourteen

She was a tough cookie. She wouldn't crumble under pressure.

Something splattered into her face. It ran from one cheek down her neck. Jocelyn tried to breathe through the swelling around her nose. Broken. She could still taste the blood at the back of her throat. Listening for signs of movement, she tried to gauge the bomber's location. Another splatter jerked her head back slightly.

"You don't have to pretend to be unconscious anymore." Shuffling scraped across what sounded like a concrete floor. There was a slight echo to it, as though they were in a large room without windows. A piercing shriek hiked her blood pressure higher as the bomber dragged a metal chair closer. "There isn't anything that's going to stop Socorro from finding you dead."

She swallowed the last globs of blood and dirt and risked opening her eyes. To pitch darkness. Pulling at her hands cuffed at her lower back, she gauged her abductor had zip-tied her. Twice. Less chance of breaking through the plastic. Something wet and cold seeped through her cargo pants and spread down her shirt. "Well, that just makes me feel special."

His low laugh wasn't villainous enough to trigger her nervous system, but it didn't fit, either. "You always had a way of making me laugh."

A lantern lit up the entire enclosed space. Cement floor, cement walls, cement ceiling. Another ping of water slipped down her face from the leaking pipe overhead. This place… She'd been here before. There was a slight charred smell sticking in her lungs.

The bomber leaned forward, letting the small source of light catch one side of his face.

Recognition sucker punched her square in the chest. "You."

"Me." There wasn't any pride in that aged expression. No sense of victory in his voice. Just a statement of fact.

"I don't understand." Shaking her head, Jocelyn tried to make every piece of this investigation fit into place in mere seconds. "The reports… They all said you were dead. That there was no way you'd survived that car bomb."

Andrew Trevino. The Ponderosa chief of police—alive and well—settled back in his chair. He'd aged significantly, or the months since his so-called death had been far crueler than she could imagine. Scar tissue shadowed across the backs of his hands. The skin hadn't just aged but smoothed into rivers in some places and valleys in others. Chemical burns. Nitroglycerin?

"Reports can say a lot of things and leave out others depending on who's writing it," he said. "It's all a matter of perspective, don't you think?"

"How?" Jocelyn pressed one hand flat against the wall at her back. Looking for something—anything—that might help get through the zip ties. Though without the use of one arm she feared she was only drawing out the inevitable. Still, she wasn't going to let her body be used to spark a war between the cartel and her team and Alpine Valley PD. She rushed to resurrect the details of that incident, a bombing of a chief of police's vehicle. Authorities had attributed credit to the Ghost. "You built the bomb and blew up your vehicle, using Marc De Leon's recipe. You faked your own death."

"You military brats are a lot smarter than I expected, especially one assigned logistics." Trevino hauled himself out of the chair. For a man closing in on his late fifties, he was surprisingly agile. No hints of wear and tear. Then again, one needed to be in tiptop shape to take on an entire drug cartel.

"Am I supposed to take that as a compliment?" Jocelyn took advantage of whatever he was doing on the other side of the room. Raising her wrists as one toward what felt like a mass of cement at her lower back, she clenched her jaw against a scream. Her abductor had removed her sling and strong-armed her wounded arm behind her back while she'd been knocked out cold. And now the pain had immobilized her altogether.

"Take it however you want. Doesn't matter to me."

He stepped outside of the pool of white light given off by the electric lantern. "Not much does anymore."

He was stalling. To what end? Didn't matter. If she had any chance of avoiding a war, it was because she got herself out of this insane frame job.

Jocelyn rolled her lips between her teeth and bit down to pull her brain's attention away from her shoulder. Sweat combined with whatever was dripping from the leaking pipe above and soaked into her shirt's collar. "You wanted authorities to believe Sangre por Sangre had ordered Marc De Leon to kill you."

"That was my first mistake." Trevino came back into the weak circle of light, though her senses still weren't adjusting to make out what he'd brought back with him. "Believing one soldier's arrest could make a difference. Believing I could inflict any kind of damage against an organization like that, but it wasn't enough."

A thread of regret laced his words. Similar to the way Baker's voice had changed when he'd trusted her with the loss he'd suffered at the hands of the cartel. Her insides twisted to the point it was hard to take her next breath. "They took someone from you. The woman Alpine PD hasn't been able to identify."

"That's what the cartel does, doesn't it? They take and they take until there's nothing left and nobody willing to stand up and fight against them. They spread their misery and violence into whatever town isn't strong enough to fight back with claims they're offering protection against bastards just like them, but it's all a lie." Trevino dropped his chin to his chest, staring down into whatever item he had in his hands. Still impossible to make out. "My daughter was one of the first to speak out against them when they started selling their poison in the high school. All she wanted to was to make our town safe enough to raise my grandkids while keeping an eye on me. Always said I was no spring chicken."

Dread pooled at the base of Jocelyn's spine. "Marc De Leon was sent to kill her."

"No. He didn't just kill her." The grief and sorrow in his voice was gone, replaced with a hardness she expected of a serial bomber instead of a chief of police desperate to protect the people he cared about. "He tortured her. For hours, right in front of me. He'd beaten me senseless. I couldn't do anything to help her except hear her beg me to save her. And after De Leon had strapped an explosive device packed into a Kevlar vest to her and detonated it, he said he'd come for my grandkids next if I kept coming for them."

Jocelyn pressed her skull into the wall behind her to keep her senses engaged in the moment. Investigators would've known about his daughter's death at the time of the bombing that had supposedly killed the chief. Why hadn't it come up in the past few days? The answer solidified. Because both his and his daughter's deaths had been blamed on the cartel. "So you faked your death."

"Victims die every day at the hands of Sangre por Sangre. The prosecutor's office can't keep up, but the truth is they can't do a damn thing to get justice for my daughter or others like her." Trevino took his seat in front of her.

Baker's sister infiltrated her thoughts, and suddenly Jocelyn was seeing Alpine Valley's chief of police in front of her. Beaten by the years of injustice, desperate to do the right thing, to make the cartel pay. Her heart hurt at the idea, but there were too many similarities between the man in front of her and the one she'd lost her heart to.

The words bubbled up her throat. "But the death of a police chief would get their notice—only Fire and Rescue never recovered your body. So you set about framing the cartel for as many crimes as you could. First with destroying evidence in Marc De Leon's murder case. Then by trying to add Baker Halsey's name to their victim roster."

"I have to admit, I didn't expect Halsey to team up with you, though." The chief's silhouette shifted, losing its caved-in appearance in the limited light. "You've certainly made my job a lot more difficult than I expected. I mean, you two just refuse to die, but then I had another idea. All this time I've been exhausting energy and resources trying to take down Sangre por Sangre alone when there is a high-skilled, highly funded organization equal to the very cartel I want gone."

"Socorro." Her mouth dried despite the building humidity inside the windowless room. "And Marc De Leon? You killed him for what he did to your daughter."

"Son of a bitch got a promotion to lieutenant after

that night," he said. "Took me weeks to find him. Thousands of dollars paid in bribes. Nobody wanted to talk. They called him the Ghost. All I had to go off of was pieces of the explosive device in my daughter's chest cavity, but my patience paid off."

Jocelyn strained to angle her wrists against the protrusion from the wall, but her shoulder wouldn't budge. "You found him."

"The bastard didn't even know who I was. Though to be fair, I didn't give him a whole lot of time to recognize me seeing as I was there to kill him." A hint of giddiness contorted the man's voice. And right then she saw the difference between him and Baker. The man she'd fallen in love with wouldn't have let his revenge get this far. "I had everything set up perfectly. Then you and Chief Halsey had to spoil my fun."

Her shoulder ached at the memory of taking that bullet just before the bomb went off. "Right. Because bringing an entire cliffside crashing onto a small town is fun."

"I didn't mean for that to happen," he said. "But I wasn't going to let it distract me from what I was there to do."

"So this is the part where I come in? You leave my body for my team to find. They gather all their federal allies and exact revenge against the cartel on my behalf." The edge of the first zip tie caught on the lip protruding from the wall, and Jocelyn shoved her weight down on her wrists. "Which means you'd have to leave my body somewhere that implicates

Sangre por Sangre. Making this the cartel's abandoned headquarters."

Her brain wasn't playing tricks on her. She had been here before.

"I know what you're thinking." Trevino stood, his outline blocking the shape of whatever he held between his hands. Closing the distance between them, he kicked his chair backward to give himself room to crouch in front of her. "They'll never fall for it."

He raised the item in his hands. Forcing the Kevlar vest over her head, the Ponderosa chief effectively pinned her arms to her side and took away her chance of escape. Something vibrated against her chest, and a red light emitted from inside. "Let's just say I've thought of that."

THE CARTEL WAS on the move.

Baker secured Maverick in the back seat of the truck and hauled himself behind the wheel. The engine growled to life at the push of a button, and within seconds, he, Jones and two Alpine PD deputies were charging after the armored caravan.

There was only one place he could think of for them to go this far out in the middle of nowhere. Their failed half-constructed headquarters. It was the perfect epicenter for the oncoming fight. Jocelyn was there. He could *feel* it.

Jones planted one hand against the dashboard from the passenger seat. "Did anyone ever tell you you're a bit intense?"

"A few. Though most of them were under arrest

at the time." Baker wasn't in the mood for jokes, but it came easier now that he'd spent the past few days learning from Jocelyn.

"Jocelyn is a fighter. There's nothing she can't handle," Jones said. "You know that now, don't you?"

He did. Because it took a hell of a lot of strength to survive what she had. But being capable of fighting for so long didn't mean she should have to. And she sure as hell shouldn't have to fight alone.

The line of vehicles ahead disappeared off the horizon, and Baker sat straighter in his seat. "Where did they go?"

"The headquarters was built underground." Jones pulled a laptop from the back seat and brought it into his lap. "Last time we were there, the structure was burning at the bottom of a sub-level hole. The cartel planned on burying it to avoid satellite imagery."

"When was that?" Baker's mind raced with every other question, but no number of answers were going to ease the tension in his chest.

"Two weeks ago. Right after Sangre por Sangre's raid on Alpine Valley." Jones hit the keys a few more times. What was he doing? Writing his biography? "Our forward observer, Cash, tore the place apart looking for Elena and her eight-year-old brother. When Jocelyn found them, they barely made it out before the building collapsed."

"It's cartel territory." There was still a piece missing here. If he and Jocelyn were right, the bomber had set about an intricate plan to bring down the cartel by adding a second chief of police's body to the tally. But that hadn't worked. Apart from a few bumps and bruises, Baker was still breathing. Which meant... His skull connected with the headrest. "His plan didn't work. The bomber. He didn't get the response he wanted by coming after me, so he had to raise the stakes."

"The bomber wants to use Jocelyn to pit Socorro and Sangre por Sangre against each other." Jones's fingers hesitated across the keyboard. Dread settled between them in the silence. "In that case, he's going to get what he wants."

Jones turned the screen to show an expanded geographical map. The screen blinked, zooming in on a rough patch of land. Then again. A square lit up around what looked like a car. "A single vehicle parked outside the building twenty minutes ago. An Alpine Valley police cruiser." The combat controller did whatever combat operators did with satellite footage, and another image took over the screen. "This was five minutes ago."

A ring of dark SUVs surrounded the lighter vehicle. Eight of them.

"Well, at least I know where West's patrol car went." Baker checked the rearview mirror. Both deputies were in the car behind them. No sirens. No lights. He caught sight of Maverick raising that caramel-colored gaze to his and floored the accelerator. The uneven terrain threatened to knock them off course, but there wasn't anything that could prevent him from getting to that building.

A chain-link gate materialized not twenty feet

in front of them. Baker didn't bother stopping. The metal scratched and thudded over the hood of the car and threw it up into the air before crashing down to one side of the cruiser. The deputies at the back had to swerve to miss it.

"You're going to pay for that," Jones said.

"Submit an invoice to the city clerk's office." The words left as more growl than reason. Baker raced along what felt like the edge of a crater in the middle of the desert. There was a decline up ahead. He didn't bother trying to slow his approach. The cartel was already inside, had possibly already found Jocelyn. The truck's tires skidded down the incline and thrust the hood into the back of one of the black SUVs.

"Come on, man!" Jones's annoyance simply grazed off Baker.

"What? Chicks love scars." He threw the truck into Park, unholstering his side arm. Then he checked the magazine. Half-empty. But, knowing what he did about Socorro operatives, he bet Jones kept extra ammunition on hand. "I'm going to need to borrow some fresh magazines. Watch the dog."

"You realize you're not the one who gives me orders, right?" The combat operative unholstered his own weapon. "And you're an idiot if you think you're walking out of there alive without me."

"Fine. I'll get one of my guys to do it." He shoved free of the truck. "So touchy. Here I thought you might like a babysitting job." Baker handed off orders to his deputies—one to watch Maverick, the other to cover the exit.

Staying low and moving fast, they maneuvered as one through the collapsed parking garage to an entrance that hadn't been pummeled with rubble. Shadows clouded his vision the instant they stepped foot inside. It smelled of fire and death and mold the deeper they navigated through what felt like a cement corridor.

"You good?" Jones asked.

Baker waited for the flashbacks, for the paralysis. For the hollowness in his chest to consume him completely. But it never came. There was only this moment. Of getting to Jocelyn. "I'm good."

"Then pick up the pace." Jones took the lead, weapon aimed high. Low voices echoed through the hall, but there were too many directions to pinpoint their location. Pulling up short, the operator handed off a radio. "We're going to have to split up. You take the right. I got the left. Try not to get yourself killed."

"Yeah. Ditto." Baker pinched the radio to his waist and took the corridor to their right. The voices were growing louder, clearer. Slowing his approach, he angled his head around one corner. But there was no one there. He took the turn and followed the hall to the end. Dead end. He pivoted back the way he came. "Shit."

Then he heard her.

Low. The words mixed together and muted as though coming through a wall. But he knew that voice, had relied on it to keep the past in its place. Baker raised his attention to the ceiling, then brushed his palm over the wall. There. An air-conditioning vent. "Gotcha."

He felt his way around the corner and slid his hand over a door. Pressing his ear to the metal, he made a response on the other side. Baker tested the handle. Locked. Of course—couldn't make it too easy. He backed up a step. Then hauled his foot into the space beside the lock.

The door slammed into the wall behind it, and he charged inside. Weapon raised, he made out two figures in the light of an electric lantern on the floor.

"Baker!" Jocelyn tried to pull away from the wall but couldn't stand. Blood crusted around her mouth and beneath her nose. The son of a bitch had hit her.

"You are a hard one to get rid of, aren't you?" The bomber centered himself between Baker and Jocelyn. All too familiar.

"Trevino." The puzzle fit together now. The lack of a body. The motive to frame and kill Marc De Leon. Ponderosa's chief hadn't died in that car bomb as everyone believed. He'd been exacting his own revenge against the cartel. "It was you."

"Surprise." Trevino raised something in his hand. A small black box, just wide enough for a single button. A detonator. "I'd stick around for the party, but it sounds like my guests are here."

A quick assessment of Jocelyn's Kevlar vest, pulled down over her arms, told Baker exactly what that detonator triggered. She'd been strapped with an explosive—the impact of which could bring down the entire building on top of them. Not to mention kill the woman he loved. "Put it down."

"I don't think you understand, Halsey." Trevino couldn't contain the smile plastered all over his face. "I put it down, and your partner here has a much bigger hole in her chest. You see, if I take my thumb off this button, we all die. So you might want to put down the gun instead."

"You son of a bitch." Baker took a step forward. "I could've helped you."

"Helped me?" The bomber raised the detonator. "No, Chief Halsey. I'm the one who's going to help you. This is what you want, isn't it? To see Sangre por Sangre pay for what they've done? Well, this is how we get it."

"Not like this." Holstering his weapon, Baker charged forward. His shoulder connected with the Trevino's gut and slammed the bastard into the wall behind him. He grabbed for the device.

The chief threw the fist clutching the detonator. Bone, plastic and flesh knocked Baker back, but it wasn't enough to knock him down. Jocelyn struggled to get free of the Kevlar vest in his peripheral vision. One slip of that detonator and he'd lose everything all over again.

Not an option.

Baker elbowed the chief in the face. A sickening crunch filled his ears. The bomber moved to catch the blood spraying from his nose. This was his chance. Baker hooked his arm around the chief's middle and hauled the bastard off his feet. They hit the ground as one. And Baker wrenched the detonator out of the man's grip.

Air eased into his chest as he got control of the explosive, but the adrenaline had yet to fade. Baker rocketed his fist in Trevino's face. The impact knocked the man's head back against the cement. Throwing him into unconsciousness. "That's for breaking her nose."

Staggering to his feet, he faced off with Jocelyn. "You okay?"

"Yeah. I'm okay." She stared up at him, a million things written on her face, but she must've known they didn't have time to hash it now. The cartel was in the building. Their time was up. "I could use some help getting this vest off, though."

Keeping his finger over the detonator's trigger, he crouched in front of her. The vest was heavier than he'd expected. Packed to the brim. But he managed to pull it over her head and make quick work of the zip ties around her wrists.

"I guess I was the one who needed help this time." Jocelyn rubbed at the broken skin on her hands.

"Anytime, Carville." Baker offered her his hand, and for a moment, he didn't think she was going to take it, but she did. Her palm pressed against his as she got to her feet, and that instant contact took the edge off.

Footsteps and flashlights broke through the door. Unfamiliar shouts ricocheted around the room as Baker and Jocelyn raised their hands in surrender.

Sangre por Sangre. He blinked against the onslaught of light, fully aware of the device in his hand.

"I think this is the part we get on our knees and hope they don't shoot us," he said.

They both lowered themselves to the floor.

Chapter Fifteen

One of the best things in life was a warm chocolate chip cookie.

And Baker's hand in hers as they faced off with a half dozen armed cartel gunmen.

Trevino lay unconscious behind them. Water soaked into Jocelyn's pants as they waited for Sangre por Sangre to decide what to do next. What were they waiting for? One wrong move. That was all it would take to put her and Baker out of their misery. Seconds pressed in on her lungs. Everything that'd happened over the past few days had led to this. To this one moment. Was this really how it was going to end between them?

She licked dry lips, knowing what might happen if she broke her silence. "Baker—"

"I was wrong before." He squeezed her hand tighter. "About what I said to you back at the camp. I've been so angry since Linley died that I've pushed everyone away for the smallest infractions. Because I was scared. I didn't want to lose anyone else, so I shut down any possibility of letting someone influence the way I feel, including you. I've been so focused on finding a way to bring down the cartel for what they took from me that I blinded myself to the best thing that's ever happened to me. You." He released a ragged breath. "I'm sorry, Jocelyn. For everything. You deserved better from someone claiming to be your partner."

A flashlight beamed straight into her face. *"¡Silencio!"*

Her shoulder burned with the possibility of taking another bullet, but it didn't hurt as much as it had before. Jocelyn moved her opposite hand to block the sensory assault, but there was no amount of distraction that could convince her that the man beside her would be able to ignore her past. Baker was law enforcement. He witnessed the results of addictions like hers on a daily basis, and he had every reason to worry he might find her unconscious and overdosed. Because it was a possibility. This thing she carried inside her wasn't ever going to go away. And as much as she hated it, there was always a chance she'd give up the fight one day. She couldn't do that to him. The warmth given off by his touch urged her to forgive him, to let him into her world, to tell him she wanted to spend the rest of her life proving she was good enough for him. But she couldn't.

Jocelyn pried her hand from his, and she felt more than saw the collapse in his expression. "Let's just get through this."

Movement divided the semicircle of cartel soldiers in half. A single figure materialized at the back.

Male, heavily armored from the outline of his Kevlar vest. The flashlights and dim lantern did nothing to highlight his features, but there was something there she recognized. In his walk, in the way he held himself. Former military. Not born or abducted into Sangre por Sangre as most of the others had been. This one had converted to a life of violence, bloodshed and dominance of his own free will.

"Socorro has a lot of nerve showing their face here after what went down on that cliffside," he said.

The voice penetrated through her minuscule amount of confidence. Recognition filled in the shadows of the man's face. "Rojas. It's been a long time. Believe me, I wouldn't be here if it'd been my choice. Don't suppose you'd look past the fact Chief Halsey is holding a detonator that could bring this entire building down on us with the slip of his finger?"

Nervous energy rolled through the grouping of soldiers. A couple backed toward the door, eyes on the ceiling.

"You know this guy?" Baker asked.

Better than anyone. They were going to walk out of here alive, if she played her cards right. "Dominic Rojas, let me introduce you to Chief Baker Halsey, Alpine Valley PD." She nodded at Baker. "Rojas is a high-ranking lieutenant in Sangre por Sangre and a fellow baker. Though I'm not sure I would call what he does baking, really. Cookies aren't supposed to snap like biscuits."

Baker cut his attention to her, as sharp as a blade. "You realize we might die right now, don't you?"

"I knew you were going to go there, Carville." Rojas charged forward, and the lantern caught on his features. Neither Hispanic nor Chinese American, but a combination of the two. It was clear in the shape of his eyes, in the lighter color of his skin. She'd been right before. Former military—the Marines. A damn good one, too. Dominic Rojas had once been a Socorro operative named Carson Lang. And he'd taught her everything she knew about baking.

He shoved his finger into her face, but she wouldn't give him the satisfaction of knocking her off balance. "That was one time!"

"Yet it was enough for second place compared to my chocolate chip," she said.

Rojas's low laugh that didn't even own a hint of humor vibrated through the room. The lieutenant straightened. "You always were out to prove you have the biggest *cajones*, but this time might be your undoing, Carville. You think you can walk in here, insult my baking and expect I would let you leave alive?"

"That's a valid question." Baker's nerves were getting the better of him.

"To be fair, I think I was dragged in here. By him." Jocelyn tipped her head back. A groan registered from Trevino as he came around. "Recognize him?"

"Isn't he supposed to be dead?" Rojas asked.

"Seems Ponderosa didn't really lose their chief in that car bombing a couple months ago," she said. "The bombings at the station and Marc De Leon's compound? Both devices were built and detonated by him."

"Don't forget the device in my hand." Baker waved

with a half smile, but the possibility of war was still very real at this point.

Jocelyn leaned forward slightly. "Oh, right. He strapped me into that vest over there and planned to set it off with this handheld detonator. It's a dead man's switch."

"Why go through all this trouble? Did you insult his baking, too?" Rojas snapped his fingers, and two soldiers lowered their weapons, peeled off from the group and maneuvered around their lieutenant to drag the Ponderosa chief forward. They laid him and the Kevlar vest at Rojas's feet. "Because I'm starting to think he had the right idea."

"Marc De Leon tortured and killed the chief's daughter. Under orders, is that right?" Her heart tried to absorb the heaviness overtaking Baker's body language, but there wasn't anything she could do for him in that respect. Humans were tribal creatures. They craved connections and support and love just like the rest of the animal kingdom. But when that love was gone, they had to grieve on their own. She understood that now.

Rojas didn't answer, which was answer enough in and of itself.

Jocelyn lowered her arm to her side in surrender. "The chief constructed and detonated the bomb that blew up his truck to make it look as though the Ghost had targeted him, too. It gave him time to plan out his revenge. First by killing De Leon. Then by trying to frame your cartel for Chief Halsey's and my deaths."

"Starting a war between us and your employer and

anyone else your government sent after us." Registering what she'd just divulged, Rojas backed off a few inches. Then he nudged Trevino's ribs with the toe of his dust-covered boots. "It was a good plan, *amigo*. My bosses have been looking for a reason to take Socorro out for good."

Jocelyn lost the oxygen in her chest. If that was true, Rojas and his men could just finish the job Ponderosa's chief started right here, right now. Effectively eliminating any competition Rojas went up against at the next bake-off and making his loyalties clear. What had started as an undercover assignment in Sangre por Sangre would end with a target on his back from the very people he claimed as his own. Had he been Dominic Rojas long enough that was an actual possibility? Would he even have a choice when faced with blowing his cover?

"Whether that happens or not is up to you," she said.

Her pulse counted off a series of beats. Quicker than a couple minutes ago when she'd been sure they were walking out of here alive. She suddenly found herself missing Baker's hand in hers, wished she hadn't shut down that point of connection in the final seconds they had left together.

Rojas's men waited for the order, each of them all too willing to add two high-priced deaths to their belts. She could feel it in the shift of energy bouncing off the cement walls, a frenzy of battle-ready tension ripping the enthusiasm she'd tried to keep as a shield around her free.

"I'll take that detonator now." Rojas positioned himself in front of Baker, hand extended.

Baker twisted his gaze to her. Waiting.

The device in that Kevlar vest was the only thing guaranteed to get them out of this mess, but she couldn't risk starting a war between Socorro and the cartel. They'd come here to stop it. She nodded, and after a long moment, he handed it off.

"Great. I'll have one of my men bring your police cruiser around. Though you should know tips are not included in today's pardon." Rojos clutched onto the detonator as though his life depended on it. Which it did. All of their lives depended on it. "Oh, and please tell your friend Jones not to shoot me on the way out. I'd hate for our friendly rivalry to turn bloody."

Jones was here? Jocelyn sucked in a breath with the realization Baker had turned to a Socorro operative to come for her. A private smile hitched at one side of her mouth. Seemed he was warming up to the idea of teaming up with mercenaries.

Jocelyn shoved to her feet. "We're not leaving without him." She nodded to Trevino.

"He's not part of the deal, Carville." Rojas folded his hands in front of him, looking for a reason to withdraw his pardon. "He killed one of us. You know as well as I do—we can't let that slide."

And the bomber deserved that fate for what he'd done, but no amount of torture or blood was going to change the past or the pain he'd caused. Ponderosa's chief would see the inside of a jail cell. Not the inside of a flaming tire. "What if I trade for something you want?"

"You don't have anything I want," Rojas said.

That wasn't true. "Not even my chocolate chip cookie dough recipe?"

There was a slight melting of Rojas's expression. Bingo. He shifted his weight between both feet before moving out of their path. "Take him and leave before I change my mind."

Dragging Trevino to his feet with Baker's help, she called into the corridor just beyond the door. "Jones, we're coming out. Hold your fire."

The group of soldiers parted down the middle again, letting her, the bomber and Baker through. Socorro's combat controller met them on the other side, his rifle pressed against his chest, as he took in the situation. Most likely counting how many gunmen he'd have to take out personally if things went sideways. "You good?"

"We're good." Her attention shifted to Baker. Though she wasn't entirely sure what she'd said was true. At least, not for them.

They moved as a unit to keep up with Rojas's men leading them through the building's remains.

Baker hauled the bomber's arm over his shoulders. "Someday, you're going to have to tell me how the hell we just walked out of there alive."

HEATED DESERT AND blinding sunlight worked to hijack his determination.

Baker pounded his fist against the front door of

Socorro's headquarters. The past few days had taken everything he had to stay upright. Witness statements, arresting Trevino under charges, running operations at the cleanup site. And there was still a possibility Sangre por Sangre would change their mind about striking back for the death of one of their lieutenants.

He'd run through those miserable minutes in that basement room a thousand times. There was no explanation for the cartel letting them go. Both he and Jocelyn shouldn't have made it out of there alive. His brain kicked up a new memory as he stood there in the heat. Of Jocelyn in the rearview mirror, pulling Maverick into her lap as they'd driven back to Alpine Valley. She'd set her head back against the headrest and stared out the window, not uttering a single word to him.

She'd disappeared after that. Wouldn't respond to his messages or calls.

The door swung inward, and Baker took a step forward before he lost his nerve. "I love you."

The words he hadn't spoken to anyone—not his father after his mom had passed, not his sister before she'd died, not even his favorite chocolate glazed doughnut—rushed out beyond his control.

Jones Driscoll stared back at him, one hand ready to slam the door in his face. "Oh, thanks, man, but I just figured our relationship could be more of a casual thing. Not really ready for anything serious."

Baker's confidence collapsed in on itself. Great. Now the first person he'd ever said those three little words to was a smart-ass operator who'd most likely hold it against him for the rest of his life. "Is she here?"

The combat controller leaned his weight into the doorjamb, folding his arms across his massive chest. A roadblock from Baker getting inside. The humor between them was gone. Big brother—whatever that meant for a team like Socorro—was on duty, and Jones wasn't the kind of guy who could be convinced of Baker's sincerity. "She's here, but unless she gives the word, you're not coming in. We protect our own, Halsey. No matter what. There is one thing she wanted me to give you in case you showed up, though."

Anticipation undermined the guilt and shame of what he'd thrown in her face before his whole world had blown up.

Jones dipped to one side and collected an oversized paper bag from near the door. "She said she wrote the heating instructions on each of the containers and that she'll have someone run out another batch next week."

He took the offering, staring down into the perfectly packaged homemade meals. The aroma of marinara and garlic drifted from inside one of the top containers. Lasagna and bread. She'd made what looked like a week's worth of dinners, breakfasts and lunches in the space of a couple days. And despite the way things had ended between them, Jocelyn had come through with making sure he didn't have to live off of microwaved ramen.

"I get it. I screwed up." Baker stared past Jones's

shoulder. Not at anything in particular, but he saw the future he'd never thought he deserved. One filled with love instead of revenge, of inside jokes and home-cooked meals, of late nights cuddled on the couch and beneath the bed sheets. He saw him and Jocelyn. Her teaching him how to bake the lemon-cranberry cookies, of them handing out gifts to the rest of the team at Christmas, of movie nights and responding to calls together. Waking to that smile in the morning and kissing her senseless at night.

Of course, it would've been hard. Him dealing with what'd happened to Linley. Her guilt and grief over her husband... But they would've gotten through it. They would've found a way to make it work. Together. As partners.

Baker slipped his hand into his uniform slacks and produced what he'd hoped to hand Jocelyn herself. "Can you give her something for me?"

"What am I? The post office?" Jones asked.

"You're a lot more reliable in my experience." He handed off the collar and new set of tags he'd had made for Maverick. He wasn't much of a dog person, but Jocelyn was worth trying for. "Thanks."

He stepped down off the wide stone steps and headed for his patrol car with the prepackaged meals in hand. There would be other chances to see her. When she was ready. Hell, he'd host an Alpine Valley bake-off if it got her to face him, but for now, he had to accept Jocelyn needed space. From him.

"Baker." His name on her lips paralyzed him from taking another step.

He turned to put her in his sights, and damn, his entire body went into a frenzy. Though this time, he wasn't scared of losing control. This time there was no disconnect. Just Jocelyn.

She stood there covered in patches of flour down her front with a bit of egg sticking to the ends of her hair. White frosting grazed one corner of her mouth. It was obvious she'd been hard at work since they'd walked out of the cartel's headquarters. Had most likely forgone sleep and taking care of herself to process everything they'd been through with hundreds of cookies, and hell, she could probably make a few hundred more and take on the entire cartel given the determination in her expression.

"Why did you do this?" She flipped the collar over her uninjured hand, running her thumb along the strands.

"Maverick's tags didn't have an updated address on them. I figured if he gets lost or separated from you like he did after..." The bag in his hand got heavier every second this distance stayed between them. That was what she did to him. Made everything feel lighter. At first, he'd resented her attempt to bring any kind of lightness into his life, even if it'd been in the shape of a cookie. But now, he couldn't go another minute with this impossible weight. "Anyway, I thought it'd be easier for someone to make sure he got home."

"That's sweet. Thank you." Her voice remained even, but there was no enthusiasm to go with it. Tucking the collar into her cargo pants, she ducked her chin to her chest. Pulling away.

And he couldn't take it anymore. Couldn't let what they had slip through his fingers like he had the past two years. Baker took a step forward. "I love you."

"What?" Her gaze snapped to his, lit up by the sunset striking her head-on. The brown of her eyes turned iridescent, otherworldly and compelling in a way he'd never seen in anyone else before. Because Jocelyn Carville wasn't like anyone else.

"I wanted to say it earlier, when we were coming back from the cartel headquarters, and then I accidentally said it to Jones a few minutes ago." He was getting off track, and his nerves were about to toss him behind the wheel and launch him back to Alpine Valley, but he wasn't going anywhere. Not without her. He was done running. Done not letting himself feel. Done with trying to burn the world and everyone in it. "My point is I love you, Joce."

Her mouth quirked to one side. "Does Jones feel the same way about you? Because I'm not sure how I feel having to compete against someone on my team."

"No. Not even a little bit." The pull they'd shared throughout the investigation took hold, and Baker dared that next step toward her. "Jocelyn, I was nothing but a ghost living in this body before you barged into my station with a plate full of cookies. I'd lost everything I thought I cared about to Sangre por Sangre, and all I wanted was to stop feeling. For people to leave me the hell alone so I could find the bomber responsible for my sister's murder. I took the chief of police job to protect the town I love from the cartel, but after everything that's happened, I realize I was just like him. Trevino. I let myself become consumed to the point I forgot what it felt like to be happy. Until you gave me a reason to look for silver linings."

Her smile was gone. Instead, a deep sadness had taken hold. Jocelyn swiped at her face, then stared into the setting sun cresting the mountains in the west.

It wasn't enough. What he'd said wasn't enough. The realization constricted his heart, and Baker tried to block the emotional response lodged in his throat, but there was no use. He was going to lose her. He understood that now. "I know I hurt you. The things I said... I wish I could take them back, but I can't. All I can say is I'm sorry, and if you give me the chance, I will spend every day of the rest of my life proving that I believe in you and that I truly love you."

She took a step down, then another. Jocelyn closed the distance between them, sliding her palm over his chest. His heart beat so hard, he swore the damn thing was trying to reach her. Problem was it already belonged to her. Every inch of him was hers. He wasn't sure when it'd happened, but there was no denying it now.

"I need a partner, Baker," she said. "Someone who knows me inside and out, who's willing to talk to me when this demon tries to take over. Because it will. I need someone who doesn't just love and accept the person I am now, but all the different versions of myself. Past and future. Who's willing to work on his own pain while doing the best he can for the people he cares about."

"I want to be that someone." Baker dropped the bag of food at his feet, threading his hands around her waist and pulling her against him. Right where she belonged. "Whatever it takes. Forever."

"Good. Because I love you, too. More than anything." The smile he'd come to love stretched her mouth wide as Jocelyn leaned in to kiss him.

A tritone sounded a split second before a frenzy of paws, fur and slobber slammed into him. Baker lost his hold on Jocelyn as Maverick tackled him to the ground. The German shepherd licked at his face and neck, settling all one hundred pounds on Baker's chest. Low playful groans accompanied Jocelyn's laugh.

She stood over him, unwilling to help as the dog wrestled him into the dirt. "I forgot to tell you. You'll have to fight Maverick for the other side of the bed."

* * * * *

SPECIAL EXCERPT FROM

⬧HARLEQUIN
INTRIGUE

Read on for a sneak preview of K-9 Shield, *the next book in Nichole Severn's miniseries New Mexico Guard Dogs.*

People were—or they became—what they pretended to be.

And Maggie Caddel had been pretending for a very long time.

Plastic cut into the sensitive skin of her wrists. She wasn't sure how long she'd been here. Getting dripped on from a leaky pipe overhead, told when she could eat, when she could stand, when to speak. Her tongue felt too big for her mouth now. Thirst did that. She'd pulled against the zip ties too many times to count. It was no use. Even if she managed to break through, there was nowhere to go. Nowhere she could run they wouldn't find her.

A thick steel door kept the animals out but kept her in. Maggie shifted away from the cinder block wall. She'd somehow managed to fall asleep, even with the echoes of shouted orders and footsteps outside her door. Another drip from above ripped her out of sleep. It splattered against the side of her face and tendriled down her neck.

This place… It held an Aladdin's cave of secrets she'd worked the past year to uncover. But not like this.

Not at the expense of ten American soldiers dead. And not at the expense of her life. The war waging between the federal government and the New Mexico cartel Sangre por Sangre had already cost so much.

A metallic ping of keys twisted in the lock. Rusted hinges protested as the door swung inward. El Capitan framed himself in the doorway. His eyes seemed to sink deeper in their sockets every time they went through their little routine. His irises darker than should be possible for a human. If that was what he was. Judging by his willingness to interrogate, torture and starve a random war correspondent, Maggie wasn't sure there was any humanity left.

She set her forehead back against the wall. It was starting again. The questions. The pain. She wasn't sure her legs would even carry her out of this room. "I'm guessing you didn't bring me the ice cream sandwich I asked for."

It'd been the only thing she could think of that she wanted more than anything else in the world. Other than being released.

El Capitan—she didn't know his real name— closed in. Strong hands pulled her to her feet and tucked her into his side. The toes of her boots dragged behind her, and it took another cartel soldier's aid to get her into the corridor.

The walls blurred in her peripheral vision. She'd spent the first few days memorizing everything she could. The rights and lefts they took to the interrogation room. The stains on the soldiers' boots, the rings they wore, the tattoos climbing up their necks. El Capitan, for instance, wore the same cologne day-to-day. It was overly spicy and would ward off demons in a pinch, but the ski mask that usually hid his face took some of the bite out. Given the chance, all she would have to do was smell him to make a positive ID.

But he wasn't wearing the mask anymore.

Which meant he wasn't worried about her identifying him anymore.

Because they were going to kill her.

Both gunmen thrust her down into the chair she'd bled in for the past... She couldn't remember how many days had gone by. Three days? A week? They'd all started to stitch together without any windows in her cell to judge day or night by. Like she'd been kept in a basement. But this room had a small crack in the ceiling. Enough for her to know they'd dragged her here in the middle of the night.

Maggie let the sharp back of the chair press into the knots in her shoulder blades. The wood felt as though it was swelling as it absorbed her sweat, her tears. Her blood. Could crime labs pull DNA from wood? She hoped so. It would probably be all that was left of her given what she'd witnessed.

"I'm losing my patience with you." El Capitan rubbed one fist into the opposite palm. Like warming up his knuckles would make any difference against her face. "Where are the photos you took? Who did you give them to?"

Same old game. Same old results. That first day

had been the hardest, when she had no choice but to be mentally present every second, to experience every ounce of pain inflicted. But now... Now she'd learned how to step out of her body. To watch from above while the Maggie below suffered at the hands of a bloodthirsty cartel lieutenant trying to clean up the mess he'd made. "What photos?"

The strike twisted her head over one shoulder. Lightning burst behind her eyelids. The throbbing started in her jaw and exploded up into her temple. And that was all it took. To detach. Disassociate. She wasn't in the chair anymore. Some other woman was. A part of her that was strong enough to get through whatever came next. She could stand there and observe without ever feeling that man's hands on her again.

"We've been through your home. We've been through your car. Next, we'll question everyone you care about." El Capitan was in a mood today. More hostile than usual. Desperate.

Maggie couldn't help but like that idea. That he was feeling the pressure of getting results out of her. That she'd held him off this long. The Maggie in the chair was having a hard time keeping her head up. She dropped her chin to her chest. "If you get ahold of my sister, tell her I want my green sweater back."

"You have no idea who you're dealing with, do you, little girl?" The cartel lieutenant stuck his face close to hers. Even separate from her body, she could smell the cigarettes on his breath. "What we can do to you, to your family, your life. All you have to do is give me the photos you took that night and this ends. You'll be able to go home."

Home? She didn't have a home. Didn't he realize that? All she'd done over the past two years was disappoint her friends, her family, her coworkers. Investigating Sangre por Sangre's growing influence throughout the Southwest was all she had left. And she wasn't going to let them get away with what they'd done. No matter the cost.

Except no one knew she was here.

No one cared. Certainly not her ex-husband.

Not even her editor would know where to start.

No one was coming to save her.

And the photos she'd taken of that tragic night— when the cartel had slaughtered ten American soldiers and then disposed of their bodies in an ambush meant to capture the cartel founder's son—would rot where she'd hidden them. Maggie licked her broken lips, not really feeling the sting anymore. Her head fell back, exposing her throat, as she tried to meet El Capitan's eyes. Sweat pricked at the back of her neck. "It's hot. Can I have that ice cream sandwich, please?"

The lieutenant fisted a handful of her hair, trying to force her to look at him, but Maggie wasn't in that body. All he was looking at was a shell. A beaten and bloodied ghost of the woman she used to be. "Take her out in the middle of the desert and leave her for the coyotes to chew on. She's worthless."

He shoved her body backward.

Gravity pitted in her stomach a split second before the Maggie in the chair hit the floor. The back of her head hit the cement, and suddenly she didn't have the strength to stay detached from that shell she'd created. In an instant, she was right back in her body. Feeling the pain crunch through her skull, realizing the warmth spreading through her hair was blood. Her vision wavered as she tried to reach for that numbness that had gotten her through the past few days, but it wasn't there anymore. Shallow breathing filled her ears. "No. No. Don't do this. You can't do this."

"Clean that up. I want this entire room and her cell scrubbed down." El Capitan threw orders with a wave of his hand as he headed for the corridor. "Make it so no one will know she was ever here."

Two sets of hands dragged her upright. Every muscle in her body tensed in defense, but she'd lost her will to fight back days ago. It wasn't supposed to be like this. She was going to make something of herself. This story…this was supposed to change everything.

Maggie tried to dig her heels into the cement, but pieces of the floor crumbled away with her added weight. Her arms hurt. This was it. Everything she'd done to rewrite her life had been for nothing. Tears burned in her swollen eyes. "Please."

The men at her sides didn't respond, didn't lighten their grip. Didn't alter their course. They pulled her through a door she hadn't known existed in the shadows until right then. One leading directly outside.

She'd been so close to escaping without ever even knowing.

A thud registered from behind her. Then another. She tried to angle her head around, but it was pointless.

Pointless to hope El Capitan had charged back into the room with a change of mind. She was going to die.

A groan rumbled through her side a split second before the gunman at her left dropped to his knees. He fell forward. Unmoving. She didn't understand. The second soldier marching her to her death released his hold, and she hit the ground. Another groan infiltrated through the concentrated thud of her heart behind her ears.

Then…nothing.

For a moment, Maggie wondered if the head wound had caused damage to her hearing or her brain had short-circuited. Then she heard him.

"Don't try to move. You're badly injured, but I'm going to get you out of here." Something wet and rough licked along one of her ears. "Gotham, knock it off. Don't you think she's been through enough?"

A small whine—like a dog's—replaced the sensory input at her ear. A dark outline shifted in front of her. Masked. Like El Capitan, but that wasn't… That wasn't his voice.

Maggie cataloged what she could see of his eyes through the cutouts in the fabric. She'd never met this one before. She would've remembered. Her vision wavered as a set of muscled arms threaded beneath her knees and at her lower back. He hauled her to his chest, and there wasn't a single thing she could do to stop him as darkness closed in. "You're not one of them."

SHE'D LOST CONSCIOUSNESS.

Jones Driscoll brought her against his chest, back

against the wall, as he scouted for an ambush. Sangre por Sangre's half-destroyed headquarters were settled at the bottom of a damn fishbowl in the middle of the freaking desert. Any number of opportunities for the cartel to take advantage. He'd managed to take down a couple of the cartel lieutenant's direct reports back in the interrogation room, but the man of the hour had managed to escape down one of the corridors. Ivy Bardot—Socorro's founder— would give him hell for that. Months of research, of tracking Sosimo Toledano's movements, of trying to build a case for the federal government to make a move. And Jones had blown it the second he'd laid eyes on Maggie.

He moved as fast as he dared straight out into the open. Cracked New Mexico earth threatened his balance as he headed for the incline that would take him back to his SUV. His legs burned with the woman's added weight, but Gotham wasn't helping either. The husky kept cuing Jones with every hint of human remains buried in this evil place.

Low voices echoed through the disintegrating parking garage. The structure was on the brink of collapse, yet satellite imagery and recon reported an uptick in activity over the past three days. Most recently utilized as a hideout for Sosimo Toledano, identified as Sangre por Sangre's prodigal son. Heir to the entire organization if and when the feds managed to capture the big dog. Seemed Sonny Boy was trying to make a name of his own. Ever since Ponderosa's chief of police had come back from the dead for revenge against the cartel, there'd been an increase in attacks on the small towns fighting to stay out of cartel business. Homes ransacked, residents running from public parks as gunfire broke out, businesses broken into and burned to the ground—all of it leading back to a single shot caller. Sosimo Toledano. Local police couldn't keep up with the onslaught, so they'd turned to Socorro.

But what was it about this place Sangre por Sangre couldn't seem to let go of? An explosion had weakened the supports months ago, the foundation was failing, water was penetrating the walls and eroding the floors. Yet the cartel lieutenant had abducted, questioned and tortured the woman in Jones's arms. Caddel. He'd called her Ms. Caddel. No first name.

Jones backed them into the shadows at the sight of two gunmen taking a cigarette break under the overhang of the underground parking garage, staying invisible. That was his job. To get in and out of enemy territory without raising the alarm. To discern the cartel's next move and calculate their strategy before they had a chance to strike. He'd lived and thrived in combat zones for half his life, but this... He studied the outline of the woman's face highlighted by a single flare of a lighter a few feet away. This felt different. What the hell could Sangre por Sangre want with one woman?

Laughter ricocheted through the hollow cement darkness. One move. That was all it would take, and the soldiers would be on him. Which wasn't normally a problem. He lived for the fight, to be on the front

lines of defense. Just him and his opponent. Protecting a woman who'd been beaten to within an inch of
her life was a whole other story. It would be hard to
engage while worrying about whether or not she was
still breathing.

Gotham pawed at Jones's cargo pants. A low groan
signaled he'd found the scent of human remains close by.

"Shh." Pressing into Gotham's paw with one leg,
Jones hoped to quiet the husky's need for attention.
They were probably standing on an entire cemetery,
given Toledano's recent crimes against humanity. But
there wasn't anything he could do about it right now.

"You hear that?" One of the gunmen faced off
with Jones's position. Though his lack of response
said he hadn't spotted them yet. Too dark.

Gotham jogged to meet the nearest gunman. A
low warning vibrated through Jones's throat, but the
husky didn't pay him any mind. Jones adjusted his
hold on the unconscious woman against his chest in
case he had to make a jump for his dog.

The nearest gunman swung his rifle free from his
shoulder, taking a step forward as Gotham waltzed right
up to him, and a tension unlike anything Jones had
experienced laced every muscle in his body. A smile
broke out across both soldiers' faces, and the second
took a knee, hand extended. "Where'd you come from?"

Hot damn. Gotham had provided a distraction,
giving Jones the chance to get out without raising
suspicions. Jones sidestepped his position, keeping
to the wall as the gunmen searched for something to
give the dog.

Joke was on them. Gotham only ate a certain brand of dog food and jerked pig ears.

He tightened his hold around Ms. Caddel as one of the spotlights swept across her face. Matted blond hair streaked with dirt and something like liquid rust caught in his watch. Not rust. Blood. His gut clenched as he got his first real good look at her swollen eyes, the cuts along her mouth, the bruising darkening the contours of her face. This woman had been through hell. But he was going to get her out.

Jones hiked the incline he'd descended to get into the structure. Sand dissolved beneath his weight, but he put everything he had into keeping upright with an added hundred and thirty pounds. Just a little farther. He could almost see his SUV on the other side of the barbed fence in the distance. He cleared the incline and stepped onto flat ground.

A yip pierced his senses.

The sound fried his nerves as he recognized Gotham's cry for help.

He turned back. The husky was hanging upside down by one foot in the soldier's extended hand, arcing up to bite at the man's wrist. Another series of laughs drew out a full bark from his dog. Setting Ms. Caddel down as gently as possible on flat ground, he tried to breathe through the rage mixing into his blood. He might not like being weighed down by a K-9 sidekick who'd rather chase his own tail than pay attention to anything Jones had to say, but no one touched his partner.

He descended the incline, not bothering to keep

to the shadows this time around. Two armed gunmen didn't stand a chance against a combat controller
employed by the most-resourced security company
in the world.

Surprise etched onto one gunman's face as he
locked on Jones's approach. The guy unholstered a
pistol at his hip and took aim.

Jones dodged the barrel of the weapon, sliding up
the soldier's arm. He rocketed his fist into the gunman's throat. A bullet exploded mere inches from his
ear and triggered a ringing through his skull. Grabbing on to the cartel member's neck, Jones hauled the
attacker to the ground. They fell as one. He pinned
the gunman's hand back by the thumb until a scream
filled the night. The gun fell into Jones's hand as the
second soldier lunged.

The second bullet found home just beneath the bastard's Kevlar, and the soldier dropped Gotham as his
knees met the earth. The K-9's yip and quick scram-
ble to his feet let Jones know he hadn't been hurt.

Jones pressed one boot into the gunman's chest
and rolled him onto his back.

"What did your boss want with her? The woman
you were supposed to execute." He hiked the soldier's
thumb back to increase the pressure on the tendon
running up into the wrist and forearm. Once that tore,
there'd be no squeezing saline solution into a contacts
case or a trigger for the rest of his life. "Why take her?"

The resulting scream drowned out the ringing in
his ears.

"She was there!" The cartel member shoved into

his heels, trying to break away from Jones's hold, but there was no point. The harder he tried to escape, the more damage was done.

"Where?" he asked.

"I know who you are." A wheeze slid through crooked, poorly maintained stained teeth. That was the thing about cartels. Every member worked for the good of the whole, but that relationship didn't go both ways. No dental coverage. No health coverage. Just a binding promise to die for the greater good. "I know who you work for."

"Then you know I won't stop until every last one of you are behind bars." Clutching the gun's grip harder, Jones pounded his fist into the soldier's face. Bone met dirt in a loud snap that knocked the son of a bitch unconscious.

Gotham raced to Jones's feet as he stood, coming up onto his hind legs.

"This is why you're not supposed to leave my side. How many times do we have to talk about this? There are mean people in the world. Guys like that don't care how nice you are." Jones wiped down the handle of the pistol with the hem of his T-shirt and dropped the weapon onto the gunman's chest. Scratching behind the husky's ears, he headed for the incline to get the hell out of here. "Though I've gotta say your distraction was on point."

Jones pressed his palm into his ringing ear. It wasn't so much the noise that bothered him. It was the percussion. He'd bounced back before when a gun had gone off next to his head. This time shouldn't be any different, but he'd check in with Dr. Piel when he got back to headquarters.

He hiked the incline to the spot where he'd left the woman he'd pulled from the interrogation room. Only, she wasn't there. Jones scanned the terrain, coming up empty. She couldn't have just walked out of here on her own. He'd known men overseas who wouldn't have been able to string together a sentence with the injuries she'd sustained. "I wasn't gone that long, right?"

Gotham yipped as though to answer.

A pair of headlights burst to life a hundred yards past the barbed fence. From his SUV. The beams cut across him a split second before they redirected around. Jones shaded his eyes with one hand and pulled his cell from his cargo pants pocket with the other. Seemed Ms. Caddel hadn't been unconscious, after all. Clever. Then again, it made sense. A woman in her position couldn't be sure of anything after going through what she had. Trusting the man who'd pulled her out of that torture chamber most assuredly came with suspicion.

Jones called into headquarters and lifted the phone to his good ear as the first ring trilled. Then started jogging-walking to catch up with the SUV. "That's what I get for leaving the keys in the ignition."

Don't miss
K-9 Shield *by Nichole Severn,*
available April 2024 wherever
Harlequin® Intrigue books
and ebooks are sold.

www.Harlequin.com

COMING NEXT MONTH FROM

⟨H⟩ HARLEQUIN
INTRIGUE

#2205 BIG SKY DECEPTION
Silver Stars of Montana • by BJ Daniels
Sheriff Brandt Parker knows that nothing short of her father's death could have lured Molly Lockhart to Montana. He's determined to protect the stubborn, independent woman but keeping his own feelings under control is an additional challenge as his investigation unfolds.

#2206 WHISPERING WINDS WIDOWS
Lookout Mountain Mysteries • by Debra Webb
Lucinda was angry when her husband left his job in the city to work with his father. Deidre never shared her husband's dream of moving to Nashville. And Harlowe wanted a baby that her husband couldn't give her. When their men vanished, the Whispering Winds Widows told the same story. Will the son of one of the disappeared and a writer from Chattanooga finally uncover the truth?

#2207 K-9 SHIELD
New Mexico Guard Dogs • by Nichole Severn
Jones Driscoll has spent half his life in war zones. This rescue mission feels different. Undercover journalist Maggie Caddel is tough—and yet she still rouses his instinct to protect. She might trust him to help her bring down the cartel that held her captive, but neither of them has any reason to let down their guards and trust the connection they share.

#2208 COLD MURDER IN KOLTON LAKE
The Lynleys of Law Enforcement • by R. Barri Flowers
Reviewing a cold case, FBI special agent Scott Lynley needs the last person to see the victim alive. Still haunted by her aunt's death, FBI victim specialist Abby Zhang is eager to help. Yet even two decades later, someone is putting Abby in the cross fire of the Kolton Lake killer. Scott's mission is to solve the case but Abby's quickly becoming his first—and only—priority.

#2209 THE RED RIVER SLAYER
Secure One • by Katie Mettner
When a fourth woman is found dead in a river, security expert Mack Holbock takes on the search for a cunning serial killer. A disabled vet, Mack is consumed by guilt that's left him with no room or desire for love. But while investigating and facing danger with Charlotte—a traumatized victim of sex trafficking—he must protect her and win her trust...without falling for her.

#2210 CRASH LANDING
by Janice Kay Johnson
After surviving a crash landing and the killers gunning for them, Rafe Salazar and EMS paramedic Gwen Allen are on the run together. Hunted across treacherous mountain wilderness, Gwen has no choice but to trust her wounded patient—a DEA agent on a dangerous undercover mission. Vowing to keep each other safe even as desire draws them closer, will they live to fight another day?

YOU CAN FIND MORE INFORMATION ON UPCOMING HARLEQUIN TITLES, FREE EXCERPTS AND MORE AT HARLEQUIN.COM.

HICNM0224